THE
WOODS
AT DUSK

A totally gripping crime thriller full of twists

KATE WATTERSON

Detective Chris Bailey Book 2

Joffe Books, London
www.joffebooks.com

First published in Great Britain in 2022

Cover art by Nick Castle

ISBN: 978-1-80405-182-5

"All the world's a stage, and all the men and women merely players. They have their exits and their entrances; And one man in his time plays many parts."

William Shakespeare, *As You Like It*

PROLOGUE

It had been a cool evening with crimson streaks across the sky, but it was full dark now.

Rain coming. The street was quiet, the houses shuttered.

Perfect.

Lightning flickered across the sky in brilliant spiky veins.

The house was dark except for the front hall light so I let myself in quietly and pulled the door shut with a soft click.

Quiet. No movement, no sound of the television — but then again, it was late. The place smelled vaguely like tomato sauce and garlic, so apparently Italian had been on the dinner menu.

It sickened me. On a personal level, my appetite had been non-existent lately, but then again, hate does that to you.

And I hated.

It was a visceral emotion, stemming from deep within, maybe a consequence of my childhood, I couldn't be sure, but I embraced it on a certain disturbing level I don't care to examine too closely.

The real question might be do I hate them, or myself?

I don't think I'd like the answer.

The gun was in the pocket of my coat and I took it out, slipped off the safety and went silently up the stairs.

This would be different than the last time.

CHAPTER ONE

A blink of an eye.

The car swerved too abruptly as she caught sight of the animal at the last possible second, a reflection of red eyes in the illumination of headlights, her jerk on the wheel sending her close enough to the edge of the road that one wheel caught it, and the next thing she saw was the tree.

She missed it by about a half a foot, skidding to a rocking halt.

Stephanie St. James sat there, heart pounding, trying to grasp just how lucky she'd been while reminding herself that the near disaster was entirely her own damn fault.

That animal — she thought it was a raccoon — could thank her for saving its life, and she could thank it in turn, for maybe saving hers.

She certainly knew better than to mix fatigue and alcohol.

The engine was still running but the vehicle was tilted at an angle and she wasn't positive she could back it out of the ditch. She gave it a try and luckily it wasn't deep and she was able to straighten the car out and pull it onto the grass right off the narrow county road.

It was, in a word, pitch dark. There was a moon, but it was obscured by clouds, and she really wasn't positive where she was exactly and that was again, her own fault. The plan to take back roads had certainly backfired. With hands still shaking from her near miss, she checked her phone for the GPS, but her signal was weak. It was no wonder, since farm fields and woods were all that were around her. An occasional farmhouse or cabin, yes, but off the road. It was getting late, close to eleven o'clock. She hadn't seen a lit window in miles.

There was no way she was driving off. First of all she wasn't sure exactly where she was other than she had the number of the narrow county road and obviously she'd taken a wrong turn at some point. But the real reason was — and she had come to this conclusion a little late in the game — she had no business driving.

Not worth the risk.

Well aware of *why* she'd overindulged without really noticing it didn't change that she had, and was now currently stuck in the untenable position of having to figure out how to get home.

Calling Anna was not an option. As a matter of fact, she wasn't going to call anyone who was remotely a colleague, no matter if they were close friends or not. She'd call her sister, but she knew her brother-in-law was out of town and Lara had two toddlers, so that was also not an option.

In short, she was stranded.

To her surprise, this late on this quiet road, she saw lights coming toward her. While she had turned the engine off her lights were still on.

To her dismay — just her luck — the vehicle pulled over and stopped.

Not her night all the way around.

The man who got out and walked over wore jeans and a light-brown leather jacket.

She never would have rolled down her window except as a testament to her extremely ill-fated evening, he pulled aside his coat and showed her a badge clipped to his denim shirt.

Really?

There wasn't much of a choice, and yes, she looked at his vehicle and believed it was an unmarked police car.

Her inner voice uttered a very bad word before she rolled down her window and at least tried for a smile.

"I'm Detective Bailey with the sheriff's department. Car trouble?" His tone was pleasant and decently concerned.

To lie or not to lie? Telling less than the absolute truth to law enforcement wasn't usually an option in her mind, but she'd just had a desperately uncomfortable evening, so she opted for the former. "Yes. I've called for a tow truck, he said it might take a little while but he'd be along."

Now she was compounding her sin. Second lie already.

"I'm hardly a mechanic but I can take a look."

She essayed a smile. "I've been having trouble with it. A light came on and it died as I pulled over, and when I turn the key, there's nothing. In the dark I can't imagine there would be much you could do. I'll just wait."

His expression was hard to read. "How long?"

"For what?"

"The tow truck."

No question, she was not at her best. "An hour or maybe a little longer." She just conjured up a plausible time frame.

"Is someone coming to pick you up?"

"I haven't gotten quite that far yet." Finally, that was true.

He paused for a moment, and then ran his hand through his hair. "Look, I'm off duty but I'm hardly going to just leave you here alone at this time of night. Give me just a minute."

This was not getting any better. Stephanie shut her eyes for a moment, and wondered if she was already paying for the lies . . . it seemed like it.

She'd only partially rolled the window down, and she heard him say, "Dispatch, this is Bailey. Can you please do me a favor? I have a stranded motorist and want her to know I am law enforcement. She seems nervous. Can you please describe me to her?" He turned to her and held out his radio.

A disembodied voice said, "This is Darlene Hutchins with the county sheriff's department. Uhm, sweetie,

Detective Bailey is a tall man with blond hair, blue-eyed, and he's not hard to look at, if you get my drift. Nice broad shoulders, too, jeans and cowboy boots usually. He has this cute little dog and when he is out and about, he sometimes takes it with him."

"Thank you," Stephanie replied ironically, not sure what else to say or why that was even necessary.

She found out quickly enough as the man in question was apparently quite to the point. "I have a cabin not ten minutes from here and that was where I was headed. I'll give you a lift there and we can wait for whoever comes to rescue you. To me it would be much better than both of us sitting here. Even if I wasn't a police officer I would not leave you by yourself at the side of the road alone. So if you don't mind, for the sake of both of us, come with me?"

There was no question she wasn't perfect with false-hoods, but if she wanted to hold with the line that she had car trouble, maybe she should consider it.

If she would just pay to have her car towed for no reason that was fine. A strange man and a remote cabin somewhere . . . it didn't sound like a good idea, but neither did sleeping in her car on the side of a deserted road until she was sure she was able to safely drive home.

Entirely her fault.

"I appreciate your concern. The rest seems accurate enough, but I don't see a dog."

He laughed with the first hint of humor in a less than humorous situation of her making. "I'll go get her. She's like carry-on baggage. I can tuck her under my arm no problem. We will be right back."

* * *

Chris Bailey doubted his unexpected guest thought much of the weathered structure in the shrouded surroundings of woodland. He had to agree it was unprepossessing, but then again, it was very nearly the middle of the night. In the light

5

of day it had a sort of rustic charm. The setting, on a river running through the woods, certainly was perfect in his opinion.

His last big case had involved a cabin of a very different sort on a big lake, but it had made him appreciate the advantages of a scenic view and the chance for a little solitude for contemplation. So he'd looked around and finally settled on this place and made the purchase.

It was absolutely quiet except for the gentle sound of the water moving in the background, the night holding a fall chill in the air. The young woman shivered as she went down the steps to the cabin, drawing her lightweight dress coat closer. He opened the door he never bothered to lock and flipped on the lights, illuminating the plain interior which consisted of a combination of living area and kitchen, and the doors to two tiny bedrooms and a single small bathroom. In one corner sat a woodstove and it was cool inside as well, so first order of business was to build a fire. Luckily he was religious in leaving the wood stacked and ready to go, with kindling and matches at hand.

"Have a seat." He gestured at the small table and chairs. "This will only take a minute or two."

He went to work with satisfying results as the flame jumped to life, waited a moment to make sure it was going to take, and then shut the glass door and stood, brushing off his hands.

When he turned around he was able to take a good look and make an assessment of his visitor. Smooth fair hair past her shoulders, thirty or so, strikingly pretty in a fine-boned delicate way, long-lashed dark-blue eyes, minimal cosmetics. He'd noted her medium height when they had walked in together from the truck. She was dressed for someplace much more elegant than where she sat now — sheer stockings and expensive pumps, the very nice coat over a blue silk dress that matched her eyes — and from the make of her car, he'd guess she had a professional occupation. She was composed, but extremely uncomfortable, and he thought he knew why.

His little dog that he'd christened with the nickname "the moppet", had quite naturally decided to settle next to their unexpected guest's chair, since she seemed to naturally take on the role of guarding the most vulnerable person in the room even though as a guard dog, she was less than frightening. Long hair perpetually in disarray, big eyes, and her pedigree was certainly in question.

"Would you like a cup of coffee?" He moved toward the kitchen and without an answer pushed a button on the machine to get the water heating.

In a faint voice, his guest said, "Yes, thank you."

"I'm afraid I drink mine just black and I might be able to dig up some sugar, but otherwise I just use this place on the weekends, so the refrigerator is generally empty. No milk."

"Black is fine."

He took out a mug from the antique cabinet in the kitchen that was the sole source of storage besides a few handmade shelves and put the coffee maker to work. "So are you a doctor or a lawyer? One of the two I'd guess."

That won him a look from those remarkable long-lashed eyes. "Why do you think that?"

"Some kind of a professional. You drive a very nice car, your demeanor, and the fact you definitely made the right decision and pulled off the road rather than continue to drive under the influence. Wise choice, because you don't want to lose a license. A stockbroker could care less. You do."

She stared at him in consternation and swallowed visibly, the muscles in her slender throat rippling.

"You weren't happy to see me stop, you didn't want me to try to start your car, and you haven't yet tried to call anyone. I hope I have some deductive skills given my profession. Relax, I never saw you driving, I am not going to give a field sobriety test because I really don't do that kind of duty anymore, and instead have offered a cup of coffee."

"Oh God." She pushed a swing of blonde hair behind her ear and sighed. "Okay, lawyer. I'm an assistant district attorney. You are correct, the last thing I want is to get in trouble when I really didn't know I was probably over the legal limit until an animal ran out in front of me and my reflexes were not exactly perfect. I'm stressed over a difficult assigned case including a triple homicide, tired too, and didn't even want to go to the dinner I had to attend, much less see my single romantic interest arrive with a date on his arm. I even sat at a table with his ex-wife. I wish I was home in my pajamas, fast asleep."

That did sound a bit like a rough evening to him.

"For the record, that's an explanation, not an excuse. I know better."

The coffee maker quieted and he took out the mug and went to set it down in front of her. "Maybe this isn't the most profound observation ever, but life gets away from you now and then."

Any DUI for someone in her position had to be reported to the Bar Association. It would be a tough and public way to get suspended or lose your license to practice.

She looked at him directly for the first time. "You're being very decent . . . thank you."

"Why wouldn't I be?" He'd intended to have a beer upon arrival, but he might have to drive her somewhere, so he decided to abstain and opted for coffee too. "You work within the parameters of the judicial system. It isn't black and white as much as we think it should be. True enough?"

"I'll agree to a certain extent."

Lawyer, most certainly, even under the influence. With wry amusement, he said, "Too much individual discretion isn't wise, I'll give you that."

"Why do I recognize you?"

"Darlene's colorful description?"

Last summer he'd handled a murder case that had spiraled into multiple investigations, and as a result of resolving those cases the story had made the national news, and much to his dismay, his picture was used along with a very brief interview because that was all he would give. The spotlight would never be his thing.

"No, though it was interesting, I'll admit that. Still . . ." She trailed off and took a sip of coffee, studying him.

He really didn't want to do it, but he supplied the answer. "That serial case tied to a prominent author. That's probably what you remember."

She might be tired and slightly impaired, but she connected the dots swiftly enough. "Oh, okay, you were the one investigating a local murder, stumbled over a cold case, and then in the course of that, unearthed some more cases that went back years. I remember all the newsfeed over it."

"That's about it."

"No big deal?"

"Part of the job."

He would bet she'd have commented more, but she'd told the truth, she did look tired.

How to handle this was out of the realm of his experience. If she wasn't who she was, he'd insist she call someone, but obviously it was a more delicate situation due to her occupation, so he thought it over.

In the end he said, "If I were you — and you are obviously free to choose however you'd like to deal with this — this place has two bedrooms. I'd just go in, lie down and go to sleep, and in the morning, I'll be happy to drive you back to your car. No middle-of-the-night calls, no explanations, and no one else needs to be involved. I am assuming you never called a tow truck."

She shook her head. "I was shaken up already by the almost accident when you came along. For the record, I am not proud of myself at this moment for lying to you."

He overlooked it. "It will not be the Ritz, but better than sleeping in your car alone on a deserted country road."

"I might just do that." Her smile was shaky. "I'm going to trust Darlene, I guess." She reached down to pat the moppet's head. "And her. She seems to like you well enough."

A young woman alone with a man she didn't know in a bad situation — Darlene must be very convincing, for she'd be an idiot to not consider the risk, and he did not get the impression, a little bad judgment aside, she was anything but an intelligent young woman.

She stood. "You've never even asked my name."

"I can't think of any reason I should." He pointed. "Bedroom there, bathroom right next door. It isn't elegant, but then again, this is a log cabin in the woods of Tennessee so elegance is not a necessity."

"Thank you again."

When he heard the door of the bedroom close quietly, he decided coffee was not the right beverage for someone with chronic insomnia considering the late hour. So he followed his original plan that hadn't taken into account a damsel-in-distress scenario, went and took a beer out of the refrigerator and sank down on the old plaid couch and put his feet up on the coffee table. As far as he was concerned, that was why it was there and it was long past the time when another scratch or two mattered. The cabin had character: worn books on handmade shelves; a plank floor; faded map of the Volunteer State framed on one wall; two antique guns in a rack made of deer antlers above the door; and an iron lamp with a beveled glass shade that could use some dusting.

Comfortable.

She didn't need to tell him her name, he had a feeling he knew it.

Triple homicide.

That didn't happen very often. Not in these parts anyway.

He was working that case.

Apparently so was she.

Life could be very ironic.

CHAPTER TWO

Once events are set in motion sometimes they spin in a direction not anticipated.

The arrest falls into that category of unexpected events. Whoever thought there would be an eyewitness. I admit I wasn't thinking clearly when I left the house, but I really didn't have a plan except to just achieve my goal.

They were dead.

Mission accomplished.

Almost.

I guess what happens next is in the hands of fate.

* * *

The hallowed halls of justice were fairly empty for a Monday morning, or at least Trey Austin could hear his footsteps echo as he walked down the long hallway. Judges' chambers at 9 a.m. sharp, though he wasn't positive he was all that sharp himself. He'd basically worked all weekend, with the memorable exception of the reception for a colleague who was just appointed to a top state position with the Attorney General's office.

He'd taken a date out of sheer self-preservation. His ex-wife was in attendance for one, and he could live without the forced small talk neither one of them cared to pretend was easy or all that friendly, but in a professional setting, necessary. Anna had stayed her distance after one askance glance, which meant the not-so-subtle ploy worked, so that was something.

There was very little room for drama in his life right now, not when he was up against the battle of his career so far and on some very unsure ground as to how to fight it.

A client who refused to explain exactly the events that led to three deaths was a difficult obstacle, and no doubt why charges would be brought even though he was a minor. The juvenile court had agreed he should be tried as an adult.

Without cooperation from the accused Trey's hands were tied, to the extent his observations on what had occurred were all he could present as evidence for the defense, and the prosecution held the advantage in every way.

Colin Simon stood stubbornly by his word that he didn't kill his family.

But he sure looked guilty.

He just as stubbornly refused to say if he had any idea who might have done it. Stony silence.

Great.

Why was the question.

The judge was at his desk and opposing counsel sat in a chair opposite when he entered. The latter had long elegant legs crossed just above the knee, a tailored jacket and a swing of blonde hair across slender shoulders.

She glanced up, and he nodded in due order at each one. "Your Honor. Stephanie."

The judge, sixtyish, spare, but at least one with a sense of humor, said affably enough, "Have a seat, Trey, and let's just get right on this."

"Yes, sir." He sat down next to Stephanie St. James, opened his briefcase and extracted a sheaf of papers. "Here's the psychiatric evaluation the court requested, done by an independent physician who specializes in adolescent behavior. Colin is a fairly normal young man as far as it reads to

12

me, no aggression, he has not altered his story that he is not guilty, never been in real trouble, is a good student, and we would like to see at arraignment that is taken into consideration when the charges are brought forth."

Stephanie St. James responded in a measured voice. "The shots were heard, he was seen leaving the house at a dead run with a gun in his hand, and there was blood in his car that matched one of the victims when the police stopped him, after I might add, many hours of searching. No sign of forced entry at the scene, and the murder weapon has disappeared, which indicates he disposed of it. The evidence speaks for itself. Eyewitnesses and he is the main and only suspect."

"He states the gun was on the floor in the hallway outside the bedrooms where the victims were found and he picked it up, not having any idea what had happened. He touched his grandmother, hoping she was still alive, and when he went to get his mother, his stepfather had evidently lived long enough to crawl out of bed and his blood was on the floor and Colin stepped in it, so no wonder he panicked and ran. He says he 'just couldn't believe it' and I quote."

"Counselor, why did he dispose of the gun?" Stephanie gave him a direct look from those dark-blue eyes he always found so striking.

He looked right back. "I don't know. All he'll say is he did not kill them. If you want my guess, he's protecting someone he thinks might be guilty. Teens are more likely to give a false confession to a crime, even one this severe, than an adult, and he isn't budging that direction. He claims it wasn't him."

He knew her. She didn't like this any more than he did. Three people dead and a seventeen-year-old boy faced with their murders. No one liked it.

"At my guess, you need to persuade your client to tell you who it might be before his arraignment." Judge Greer looked at him with lifted brows. "However, I consider everything, so I'll take a look at the evaluation."

They walked out together, and Stephanie said mildly, "I admit I am in the dark as to how your young defendant has a prestigious firm representing him, much less one of their top attorneys. As far as I can tell, Colin Simon truly orphaned himself if he's guilty."

"An interested party retained us. That's all I can say."

"Intriguing."

So was she.

Old problem for him, just a different day. Her profile was perfect and symmetrical, her shapely body draped by a silk blouse and business-like skirt, ivory and charcoal gray respectively, and discreet onyx earrings under that silky curtain of blonde hair. As usual, he did his best to not reflect his feelings in his expression. "Well, confidentiality being part of our job, you understand, I'm sure."

"Hmm. I understand that you aren't going to tell me a damn thing as long as you understand I really have no choice but to level charges at your client. He was there, he had the weapon, he fled the scene, and he tampered with evidence."

"We get each other." That was true, on a professional level. On a personal one, they weren't quite in sync.

Not yet.

"Give me someone else." Her remark was quiet, but it made him stop as she put her hand on his arm. She gave a slight grimace. "I mean it, Trey. I don't want Colin Simon to be guilty. What a waste of a young life, thrown away after three other lives were taken so violently."

"You know I agree." They knew each other well on a personal level, even though he'd become a defense attorney and she'd gone into the public sector, they'd graduated from law school only a year apart and had quite a few mutual friends, including his ex-wife, though he wouldn't characterize his relationship with Anna as friendly necessarily. Civil at best, and they both worked at it to achieve that bare minimal.

He was conscious of the light pressure of Stephanie's fingers on his sleeve. "The police seem to think they have apprehended the right perpetrator, but I just don't think they have. It's my job to give him a defense either way, but he isn't a sullen teen with a juvenile history, and the way he denies it is believable. Why he reacted like he did is a mystery, but maybe as reality sets in he'll cooperate more."

She stopped by the elevators and he did as well, even though he was heading back to the office. "Let me know, of course, if there's anything new."

"Of course."

A glance was slanted his way. "Did you enjoy the reception Saturday night?"

Might as well tell the truth. He shrugged. "No, not particularly."

"Me either." Her smile was tinged with irony. "I did meet someone interesting, but other than that, it was not an evening I'd care to repeat." The doors opened and she stepped into the elevator. "Keep me in the loop."

He stood there for a moment as the doors closed, and stifled an inner curse.

"Hey, Austin."

When he turned he saw Richard Dorset was in the hallway, his tie a striking verdant green statement against his black suit and red shirt, but he carried it off in style as usual. They were in the same firm. Trey said mildly, "Nice ensemble. Did I miss Christmas?"

"How long have I been telling you that you're entirely too conservative?" Rich looked unperturbed as he walked up, his expression amused, his hair immaculate as usual. "Grays and navy blue almost exclusively. You look like a lawyer."

"I am one." He was unwillingly amused.

"So am I, I just let my adventurous spirit shine through. Tell me something; why not just ask her out?"

The question actually touched a nerve, though he didn't really want to admit it. Nor could he pretend he didn't understand the inquiry. He'd been the idiot standing there staring at those closed elevator doors. "Stephanie?"

"For God's sake, Austin, the only person that doesn't see it is her. Transparency takes on a whole new meaning with you."

"Maybe I'm shy."

Or maybe she was deliberately overlooking it. *Reason number one to not ask.*

"Right. I've been in court with you, shy doesn't apply."

They were colleagues but also friends and Trey gave him a sardonic look. "You know full well Stephanie and I have a past that includes me standing at the altar with her as the maid of honor right there at my wedding — while I swore until death do us part to her best friend. How did that work out? Maybe that's why."

"Not every relationship works, and it usually is a street that runs both ways. Stephanie is intelligent, she knows the score, so that means you are selling her short, my friend."

"Am I?" It wasn't like he didn't know the statistics on divorce. He just didn't ever want to be someone on the wrong side of that percentage. He took a moment and said calmly, "I get where you are coming from but I don't know if it makes a difference one way or the other."

"No further comment. I'm headed to the second floor. Since you are standing right there looking all forlorn and dejected, do you mind pressing the button for me?"

"Forlorn? Fuck off, Rich."

He pressed the button, laughing even though it wasn't really all that funny. He wished it wasn't true.

But it was.

* * *

The restaurant was quiet, with low music in the background so muted she couldn't make out the melody, and nothing else but the occasional laughter or clink of silverware. It was the very beginning of the lunch crowd trickling in but the only time she could manage. To say her schedule was full was an understatement.

"Was Trey there?"

Anna Hernandez glanced up from contemplating her glass of iced tea, looked at her mother and lifted a brow. "Where?"

"At the reception Saturday night, of course. You are pre-occupied today."

She was definitely distracted. No argument there. Her tone was even when she replied. "Did you think for a minute he wouldn't be? By the time he's in his mid-forties he'll be a federal judge or even the Attorney General of the State of Tennessee, trust me. He has never been less than aware of how to handle his career, so yes, he was there."

With a shapely brunette she didn't recognize, but that actually didn't bother her. They were noticeable together, his striking dark good looks always turned heads and there was no surprise on her part to see him with a knockout, but she happened to know that whoever that woman had been, it was probably only a passing interest on his part.

"He'll be good at either one, judge or AG."

"True. He's got that Hollywood face going for him, but even in my most vindictive moment I can't say that accounts for where he's at or where he's going. Is there some point to this?"

Her mother just shrugged. "I've seen his name because of that new homicide case so I was thinking about him."

There was no question that Maria Hernandez was never going to understand why Anna had filed for divorce from someone like Trey Austin, and she wasn't about to explain either.

It had been a year since the paperwork had gone through and she'd gone back to her maiden name and picked her life back up. The adjustment hadn't been very easy and there were limits to her desire to hash through the personal aspects of why it hadn't worked out.

So, discussion over, or at least that side of it. On a professional level, at the moment she couldn't disconnect from her ex-husband if she tried.

An untenable situation had arisen whether she liked it or not. It was ironic, to say the least, with Stephanie prosecuting, Trey defending, and the responsibility for the well-being of a child in serious trouble solidly on *her* shoulders.

An unholy trinity if there ever was one.

"Yes, well, speaking of that case, Colin Simon is a minor right now without a guardian, and so his file has landed on *my* desk. He's still in juvenile detention, but his lawyer — yes, Trey — has contacted our office to say they expect him to be able to make bail so social services has to decide what to do about a minor charged with murder. I'm currently mystified as to how it is possible for a seventeen-year-old boy to make bail as I guess it will be really steep, but then again, I don't have any idea how he could retain a high-powered attorney either."

Her mother stared at her. "Are you serious?"

"I wish I wasn't."

"What are you going to do?"

"My job. It's true enough while Steph and Trey were bound to cross paths frequently, I have to say I never thought I'd be stuck in the middle of one of their cases, but I am, and so it goes. Colin is innocent until they prove otherwise, so he needs an advocate."

"What foster parent would take him in? It is possible he murdered three people."

That was a valid question. "I admit I've never handled a situation like this one before. We're talking to the state services on proper placement protocol." She paused. "It depends on the exact charges. It is possible if the prosecutor thinks they can prove premeditation, first degree will be on the table. Colin's eighteenth birthday is in a few months."

"Is Trey worried about that?"

Their food arrived at that moment so she didn't have to point out that Trey had no obligation to tell her what he had in mind for a defense for his client, nor did she really have a right to ask. She picked up her fork and speared a piece of shrimp from her salad. "I have no idea. Believe it or not, we don't have heart-to-heart talks any longer."

Or maybe they never really had, and it was part of the problem.

Her mother was a pragmatic person, even if they didn't always see eye to eye. "You will work together for this young man. And as for Stephanie, I trust she wants justice, not just an easy conviction."

"Of course she does. You know Steph."

"I certainly do. That is, I know the lovely young woman." Her mother's smile was uncertain. "I don't know the prosecutor. He's only seventeen. Surely she'll keep that in mind." She added softly, "That's so young."

Shit. That was what this conversation was about. Anna's cousin Tony had been killed in a car accident at that same age, and her aunt was still for the most part a non-functioning human being because she just couldn't cope over a decade later with her son's death. The trauma of it resonated through their close-knit family to this day, making every holiday gathering not a celebration but instead an uncomfortable event Anna avoided as much as possible. She'd actually been grateful for the cold she'd had over last Christmas so she didn't have to invent an excuse to stay home and skip the not-so-festive festivities.

"It isn't the same thing, Mom," she said quietly. "An accident is quite different, but I understand what you mean, don't get me wrong."

"I just think about young lost lives and wish I didn't know how it feels."

Unfortunately, Colin Simon didn't have any family left to grieve his loss if he — and that still was an if — really was the guilty party and was locked up for life, and it would be his own damn fault.

To be a helpless onlooker to events she couldn't control was an unwelcome but increasingly familiar part of her life and Anna wasn't going to sit passively by and let it happen.

Again.

She said firmly, "I'm his voice and I'll make sure everyone hears it."

CHAPTER THREE

The weapon hasn't been recovered. The waiting is an interesting feeling, knowing it is out there and should someone stumble across it that event could change my life.

I personally have no idea where it might be now.

* * *

This should be an easy call, but one never knew.

Chris had come alone and that was his partner's choice. Carter opted out, and probably was just as well considering the venue. First of all, his partner always wore a jacket and tie and that did not always sit well in this neck of the woods, but Chris usually wore jeans and boots and a casual shirt, because his boss let him get away with it and it was more comfortable. The unspoken agreement was probably because the sheriff was a canny man and realized that some people in this part of Tennessee did not trust men in suits when they came knocking on their door.

Bailey trusted nothing to fate, and very few people, so he walked up the broken cement walk cautiously and he assumed nothing. Just because the shabby farmhouse appeared deserted didn't mean it was, and sure enough as soon as he gained the weathered front porch he heard a distinct thud from inside.

He knocked, not demandingly, but with authority and there were no illusions over whether his arrival had been observed or not. The only question was whether or not the door would open.

So much easier if it did, he mused in resignation. He wanted a conversation, not an arrest.

Luckily, it did swing open, bringing with it into the cool afternoon a whiff of cannabis smoke and the muted sound of a television in the background.

The young man who stood in the doorway was visibly nervous, his bloodshot eyes and two-day scruffy beard along with torn jeans and a rumpled T-shirt not exactly giving him a well-kept appearance. "Can I help you?"

"Yeah, Randy, you can." Chris kept his tone mild. "Mind if we have a word? I'm Detective Bailey with the county sheriff's department."

"I—"

"I'm not here about anything besides Colin Simon's recent arrest."

The boy's eyes widened. "Oh shit that, yeah. I still can't believe it."

"Can we maybe sit down and talk about it? You are already eighteen, so there is no need for me to talk first with your parents, but if you'd like to help him out anything you can offer in information would really be appreciated."

A polite way of pointing out he was an adult in the eyes of the law and maybe a nudge toward the inclination to do the right thing.

Randy gestured at the porch steps. "Out here okay? My dad is crashed on the couch. He works nights."

Chris was fairly sure his father was watching television and smoking weed, the latter still fully illegal in the state of Tennessee, but that was not part of his investigation. To his mind the murder of three people was more important. He gestured to the steps. "Let's sit then."

The kid looked relieved when they both took a seat on the warped top board. "Colin is a friend. I feel so bad for him. Both his parents. Man." He shook his head.

"He said he stopped by that night. Did he?"

"Yeah, he did."

"How did he seem?"

"Pretty much as usual." Randy exhaled and rubbed his forehead, then gave him a sidelong look. "We drank a couple of beers together, but I mean only a couple because that's all we had. So he wasn't drunk or anything. Do you really think he did it?"

Chris considered that question and answered accordingly. "My job is to find out what happened. Did he have problems with his parents? Did they argue often, set curfews, complain about his grades, things like that?"

"Complain about his grades? Dude, he's at the top of our class."

Carter would definitely never get called dude. Chris had to stifle a laugh just thinking about his conservative partner's reaction to that reference and overlooked it. "Did they get along to your knowledge?"

Randy at least did take a moment to think about it. "Yeah, I think so. Joe was his stepdad, but he was an okay guy and he never knew his real dad, and his mom and grandmother were really nice. He didn't complain about any of them really."

"Just an ordinary night then?"

"Yeah." A shrug accompanied that declaration. "I mean, I guess so. I didn't notice anything."

"Do you know if he had a gun or where he might get one?"

"Of his own? He never said anything to me, but as far getting one, dude, this is Tennessee in the good old USA. If you want one, you can get one. You're carrying, right?"

"I'm an officer of the law," he said mildly. "Not quite the same as a seventeen-year-old boy untrained in firearm safety. Okay then, thank you for talking to me, and I'm going to give you my card so you can call me if you think of anything that might help us to understand what resulted in the deaths of three people."

He stood and took a card out of his pocket and handed it over.

Then he said, only because the kid did seem genuinely concerned about his friend and had been cooperative, "I'm not DEA, but I do suggest, since they do fly over this county at times, for your dad to keep the amount of weed you grow to only what would be reasonable for personal use, because he really doesn't want to draw their attention. We can arrest him just for having it, but they can take you down on federal charges if the amount on your property suggests you are really a dealer."

"Well, shit." It was a mutter. "It's nothing, I swear it. A bag or two here and there."

"It's illegal and has been brought to the attention of the sheriff's department. I don't want you clogging up the judicial system, so just give him my advice, and we're square. Deal?"

Randy shoved his hands in his pockets, his smile weak. "Okay. Thanks, I guess."

He drove back to the office, thoughtful and really examining the case. If Colin was not the killer — and it seemed on the surface a slam dunk he was — then who else would kill the entire family without a robbery or forced entry? And why had he disposed of the weapon?

Carter was at his desk, a frown on his face as he worked at his computer. Middle-aged, with way more experience, he was a very conventional cop, strictly by the book. Their initial assignment to work on cases together had not exactly been smooth. They didn't share the same style, but their last case together had managed to achieve a level of mutual respect anyway.

Chris walked over and leaned a hip on the edge of his desk. "I just don't think he did it, but it sure as hell looks like he did."

23

Carter pushed a key and looked up in sardonic question. "Uh? Santa didn't eat those cookies left for him by the hearth? You're suspecting one of the elves? I know you operate on a level where you think everyone knows what you mean whenever you speak, but sometimes that's not the case. Did Randy Price give you any valuable information about the Simon case?"

He could do sarcasm too. "Apparently you do know just what I mean. The answer is, yes and no."

"Do tell."

"As far as he knew, Colin was acting perfectly normal the night it happened, home life was stable, and he didn't have a gun."

"So, nothing really valuable."

"He knows something, he just plain didn't want to tell me."

Carter leaned back in his chair and lifted his brows. "Okay, with great reluctance over the course of our professional relationship I have come to trust your gut. Why do you think that?"

"He was relieved when I ended the interview and never asked the right question evidently." Chris rubbed his jaw, thinking it over. "He was willing to talk to me, but nervous, and it wasn't the fact I pointed out before I left that our department was aware his father was growing and selling weed, it was something else."

"Just a hunch?"

"For now . . . why did that kid dispose of a gun that killed his family if he didn't murder them?"

"Protecting someone, but I have to admit it baffles me he would."

Chris found it pretty incomprehensible too.

* * *

It wasn't as if Stephanie had a very demanding social life but still, looking at crime scene photos even over a nice glass of wine was not exactly a relaxing evening pastime.

They weren't pretty.

The bar was quiet and upscale, and very close to where they both worked, which is why she'd suggested it.

"Close range," Dr. Hamblin said in a pragmatic tone, but she was a very businesslike medical examiner. "I don't speculate in my summaries, but since you are prosecuting this case, I will tell you I'd guess the shooter was not confident of hitting the target from very far away. I don't know if that opinion is relevant to the suspect or not, so consider it an unbiased observation."

It fit a seventeen-year-old probably, not a cold-blooded intruder, and there had been no sign of forced entry. "I see."

"Stephanie, you've seen the pictures before, you want to ask me something else." Hamblin, middle-aged and apparently opposed to any and all cosmetics, also had bowed to nature in that she let her gray hair thread through the darker strands, and gathered the curly mass back in a ponytail. Under the white coat she wore scrubs and had no problem ordering a martini, vodka with lemon, no vermouth.

True enough about the something else.

"The younger female victim, Roxanne Gaines, she had an unusual tox screen. I don't see how it makes a difference in the case but it does make me wonder if it has any significance. Her son is being charged with very serious crimes. I need to figure out if premeditation is involved, and at his age, it is hard to seek a murder one in this state, because we do have the death penalty. If anything is significant, before we go for arraignment, I need to consider it."

"She was on some powerful anti-depressants, true. Or at least it came back that way. Whether she was legally prescribed them is up to the investigators in your case to discover."

They had. She did have several prescriptions, but had taken twice the usual dose. The county might not have a big city, but the law enforcement on this so far seemed quite efficient.

"Would you, as a physician, say there was enough in her system that she would have slept through the entire thing?"

"I would say in court — this is what you are asking, isn't it — that probably there was, yes."

"But we can't establish who was shot first."

"It isn't possible, not by body temp or lividity because they were shot within minutes of each other."

If Colin had planned this, and known his mother wouldn't be awake for the crime . . . it would make it easier to commit the murder and not have to look her in the eye. The implication was damning, but she'd have to prove it in court. Maybe he wouldn't know she took those meds. He was seventeen.

But, very bright. A good student. It worked for Colin both ways. She could use it against him, or Trey could use it *for* him.

Of course, it could be argued that if you planned to kill your entire family whether your mother was aware at the time of the murder or not might not matter to the perpetrator.

The two detectives that she'd sat down with after the arrest both thought the stepfather had been the first target, which made sense as he would be most likely to be able to stop the shooter. Colin's mother next, and the grandmother, who was hard of hearing according to friends and neighbors who had been interviewed, had been last.

Why did he go back into the first bedroom? His stepfather had lived long enough to get out of bed, hence the bloody footprint and the blood in Colin's car. Maybe he'd heard someone moving and realized they weren't both dead.

But firing a gun in an enclosed space like a bedroom was loud enough to deafen a person. She doubted he would hear, though maybe he went back just to be sure.

Or he came home, found the gun in the hallway as he claimed, picked it up, saw his grandmother's door was open and what had happened, ran into his parent's bedroom, stepped in the blood, and then ran from the house.

With the gun.

Damn.

A lot of maybes.

She wasn't being pressured to bring a tougher charge. This was her case, but how she handled it would impact her career and conscience. If he hadn't disposed of that gun and would tell them where it was, she'd take premeditation off the table.

As it stood, since if she believed his story that meant he'd covered for someone else, Trey needed to get his client to talk or give another reason for getting rid of evidence.

She fingered the stem of her wine glass. "If I feel like Mrs. Gaines's awareness has any impact on the case, you might get called as an expert witness, but as of yet, I don't know that it will make a difference. I'm trying to establish several different scenarios right now. If she took a larger dose, why? Or her son could have drugged her — and only her apparently — for some reason, which might have been compassion."

"Shooting her," Hamblin said with all due practicality, "was not very compassionate."

"I can't disagree with that, but motive is always dicey. If you understand serial killers, give me your insight, because I sure don't."

The medical examiner's smile was humorless. "Cannot help you there, Counselor. Your young man doesn't qualify as one anyway even though there are multiple victims, but I get your point. Frustration, anger, a sense of helplessness or hopelessness; I have no idea why he'd choose to eliminate three people who supposedly cared about him. Maybe he doesn't know either."

That was what was daunting. The good doctor had a point. What if she was trying to make sense out of something that just had no rational explanation?

She finished off her wine. "If that is the case, all I want is for him to admit it, but my instincts say it isn't that simple."

"Nothing is."

CHAPTER FOUR

If it were possible to ask her, I wonder if my grandmother would still tell me that there is always a reckoning.

But she is no longer with us now, is she? So it is impossible to know if she believed that when she spoke those words — if it was just a tidbit of wisdom or a prophecy.

One does wonder. I know I do.

* * *

The request was welcome, the reason for it not so much.

Hell yes, Trey wanted to have breakfast with her, but that would be more in the vein of a sleepy cup of coffee after a very satisfying night in the same bed enjoying an activity involving mutual nudity and sexual pleasure, but that was certainly not the case.

The restaurant Stephanie suggested was a small corner diner-style place with cozy booths that had been redone to imitate the fifties. When he walked in he smelled coffee and maple syrup before he spotted her at a corner table.

Fine. She wanted to talk about his client.

Trey was up in the air over whether or not this was a good idea, or if Colin might find it intimidating, but he was certainly willing to hear what she had to say.

She looked fantastic in some sort of soft blouse that draped the curves of her breasts, a navy skirt, her hair smooth and falling past her shoulders . . . and what he really needed to do was pay attention to the conversation, which, in his defense, he normally was able to do just fine.

If she wasn't in the room.

This attraction, he decided ironically as he took an opposite seat, was penance for some sort of past sin. Childhood or even a former life, he wasn't sure. "Hi."

"Good morning. I ordered us both cinnamon rolls and coffee."

"I see that, thank you."

She was amused. "Don't look so wary."

His return smile was cynical. "Ah, when a district attorney wants to meet with you to talk about the charges against your client and bribes you with a cinnamon roll, wary is probably the logical way to approach the situation. Why are we here, Steph?"

"I want to talk to Colin directly, but of course you will be there if I arrange a meeting, so I'd like to make sure we are on the same page. He's a minor and I have never handled a case like this."

He got it. "You are trying to decide how to charge him."

"Let's talk about it without a judge present." She picked up her coffee cup. "I wouldn't mind your help with it."

"We *are* opposing counsel."

"I know. So I could use your advice."

He was required to point out: "I believe there might be an ethics conflict there, but on the other hand I agree maybe a discussion of this off the record could not hurt. Let's talk."

She looked at him squarely. "That's what I am asking for and it is in the best interest of your client. I'd like to talk to him before my office decides on the final charges, and I know, of course, you'll wish to be there for the conversation."

"You are correct." He poured some cream into his coffee and stirred it in. For some reason he could never just drink it black, not even back in college. "I'd like to know what you hope to gain from the conversation that you think he'd tell you he hasn't told the police."

"For one thing," she said dryly, "who retained you. If he is innocent like he claims, he's protecting someone and someone is evidently protecting him."

He shook his head. "The person who made sure he had an attorney is not the person he's protecting, Steph."

Her gaze was speculative. "You are with one of the most prestigious law firms in this fair state and are already considered one of the top defense attorneys in this area of the country. They didn't just make sure he had an attorney, they paid a lot of money to make sure he had a very good one."

"Thank you for the compliment." He sipped his coffee and looked bland.

"It was an observation, so don't let it go to your head. What I really want is to ascertain if I feel he is telling the truth or not on a personal level. You seem to think he is and I get the impression from the sheriff's office that they aren't completely convinced either since two detectives are still looking into it even though he's in custody. They don't seem to think they've solved the case."

"At the moment all he's charged with is tampering with evidence and fleeing the scene of a crime."

"Trey, he didn't even call 911."

"First of all, they were, even to a seventeen-year-old, clearly deceased, and second of all, I do believe if you walked in on a horrific scene of your entire family being murdered, you might be traumatized enough to not think all that clearly." He paused and added quietly, "You might even wonder if the person who committed the crimes was still there, waiting for you, so you would flee the scene and take the gun with you."

"I think I see clearly the defense you'll present and I would argue the same thing, except for one sticking point. The weapon."

He had to agree. "Yes, I'm well aware and he isn't budging, so if you talking to him makes him explain, I'm all for it. My job would be easier."

"I'd like to try it before I have to make a decision. We desperately need another suspect at least. He just looks really guilty because of the lack of forced entry, the disposal of the gun, and how he never called the police. There was residue from a fired weapon on his hand."

"Because he picked up a recently fired weapon. He admits that. All the rest of it is damning and that isn't a secret to me, but you are going to have to be able to prove intent for first-degree murder."

"If you think I don't know that, you don't think I'm a competent prosecutor. But you and I know this wasn't a burglary gone wrong, so there *was* intent. Was it his? Can one of the detectives sit in on this meeting? They've talked to him, but I want them to hear what he might tell me."

Three to one was not promising for Colin to want to talk, but truthfully, Trey hadn't had any luck so far breaking the stubborn silence.

Maybe Stephanie could convince a seventeen-year-old boy that he was in such a serious situation his future was a wasteland of closed walls and locked doors, if not worse.

In a certain sense she was the enemy, but she was also an attractive, slender female, non-threatening, and had a serene poise that served her well in the courtroom. Even her opponents generally liked her, and certainly the judges did as far as he could tell. She was fair-minded and from their brief conversation three days ago, she was more on his client's side than otherwise.

Give me someone else.

The detective sounded like a good idea to him.

Trey said, "Let's set it up."

* * *

After he checked in, passed through the check points for weapons or anything else he wasn't supposed to have on his person — Chris did get a free pass on his sidearm as a police officer — he was escorted to an interview room.

Not, it seemed, the only one who was early.

He didn't recognize the woman sitting next to the young man he wasn't quite yet sure had committed three murders, but he had talked to her on the phone.

Her dark hair was in a fashionable swing by her jawline, her fine-boned face set, chin tilted slightly upward, and even though he was definitely not the enemy in this situation, just her body language reflected she thought of him that way on a personal level.

Fine, he wasn't stunned since this was high profile. Given her position with social services as the one assigned to Colin Simon, she no doubt wasn't happy to see him.

"Ms. Hernandez." He sat down across from them.

"Detective Bailey. You wanted to meet with Colin?" Her voice was icy and professional.

"I am not here to question him again," he responded carefully. "I'm here at the request of the assistant district attorney handling the case, and with full consent from his attorney since we still have the investigation open and charges have not been filed further to the ones he's being held for."

Just to put it all in perspective, he thought grimly. *We all have to play nice.*

She did at least acknowledge that with a slight inclination of her head. "Why are we here? Do you know?"

He didn't really, but luckily at that moment both of the lawyers in question walked in.

It was part of his job to read people and he registered immediately that the antipathy from Ms. Hernandez was not directed at him.

Colin's lawyer must be the tall, well-dressed, dark-haired man because he recognized the attractive blonde female D.A. since they'd spent the night together — in an entirely platonic way. He sensed an instant tension between the other three adults in the room.

He was missing something here, but then the male lawyer said with cool familiarity, "Anna." Then he turned and offered his hand to him. "Detective Bailey, I'm Trey Austin and represent Colin."

There was no question he knew the name.

Chris shook it, a little surprised this particular attorney who had defended some high-profile clients had taken on a case like this, but that was fine with him.

Might be pro bono. The kid could use some help, no doubt about that. Chris was not having any luck in finding another suspect.

However, he was now pretty interested in why he had been invited to this party by the very pretty prosecutor who gifted him with a rueful smile and said, "Detective Bailey, nice to see you again."

* * *

When Stephanie discovered who was handling the murder case she was prosecuting, there had definitely been more than just a moment of dismay. It wasn't like he hadn't clearly identified himself, she just hadn't made the connection until she went over the reports again.

Was she glad a competent police officer was investigating this important case? Yes, she was.

Was she chagrined at her less than responsible behavior? Yes again.

Oh well, she had to own it, and all he said was, "Ms. St. James."

This was her idea, so Stephanie went first. "Colin, I'm Assistant District Attorney Stephanie St. James. My job is to try to decide how my office wants to handle the pending charges that are possibly directed at you and make you accountable for the deaths of three people, if indeed you are guilty of the crimes." She paused and added, "I want to say if you are not guilty, I am your friend."

Luckily, Trey did pick up the ball, and she knew he would or she never would have requested the meeting with him ahead of time.

"They could use some cooperation." Trey looked pointedly at his client, folding his hands on the table. "The main stumbling block you and I face is that missing murder weapon. There is a witness that saw you run out to your car with a gun. You have admitted picking it up in the hallway and the assumption is that it was the weapon used in the homicides. You had some residue on your right hand consistent with a weapon having been recently fired, but actually not really enough for it being fired six times. That supports your story."

"I didn't fire it at all."

"If forensics could be done, there is a good chance of tracing it back to the owner, especially if it was purchased legally and is registered. You need to tell us what you did with it, Colin." Stephanie was emphatic. "It would be even better if you would explain why you got rid of it in the first place. At the moment you are only charged with tampering with evidence which is why they are holding you, but more formal charges are coming unless something changes."

No response. At not quite eighteen, Colin was close to six feet tall, athletically wide in the shoulders, blond and blue-eyed — a nice-looking kid, clean-cut and so far, polite, but there was a mutinous set to his mouth at the moment. He just gazed back.

They all waited.

Anna turned to the young man and lightly touched his shoulder. "I can honestly say she wants to help you and so does Trey. I'm here to make sure your rights are protected, but if you want advice, I'll give it. I'm not a lawyer with an agenda. I'm an adult voice to speak for you."

"I didn't kill them." Colin's voice wavered and broke and he swallowed and looked at Trey. "I didn't. That should be enough. Isn't it true they have to prove I'm guilty? And I'm not."

"Beyond a reasonable doubt is our issue here. The question is going to remain why did you dispose of evidence?" Stephanie stayed patient, because there was no choice really.

Trey had enough to work with, and without the damning loss of the gun in the triple shooting, he could make a very solid defense case. Joe Gaines's two guns had been found in the dresser in the bedroom, untouched.

"I never said I did."

Stephanie looked back and her expression was neutral. "I know, and I have gone over your statement, but I'd like you to tell *me*. What happened that night?"

"Ms. St. James is the one who decides if and how the court will level charges at you," Trey said. "This is important, Colin. Be clear and truthful."

"I've *been* truthful."

Stephanie merely lifted a brow. "Then be truthful again. I would appreciate hearing it directly from you."

Anna gave her two cents of encouragement. "They wouldn't ask if it wasn't necessary. They do understand it is painful."

Colin exhaled audibly, and then shrugged. "Okay, okay. I got home from hanging out with a few friends. I went in and the house was dark. I turned on the lights and went upstairs. There was a gun lying in the middle of the hallway, which, of course, wasn't normal, and my grandmother's door was open, and that wasn't normal either. I went in and saw the blood . . ." He faltered and stopped, but rallied. "And I couldn't believe it. I ran to tell my mom and Joe, but then . . . there was nothing I could do, because they'd both been shot too. I don't really remember having the gun, but I must have picked it up. I didn't know where whoever did this could be, so leaving the gun there was a bad idea might have been what I was thinking, I really don't remember. I just needed to get out of that house."

Stephanie nodded, and that was right in line with his initial story after he was finally picked up, hours later. She asked, "Where did you go?"

"I drove around. I think I just drove around . . . I was kinda numb. It was like a bad dream or something. I was trying to understand it . . . I don't know."

"What did you do with the gun?"

No immediate answer.

In the end, Colin just shook his head.

"You don't know or you won't say?" Stephanie was nice, but she wasn't going to let him slide either. "If it is the latter, can you tell me why?"

"No."

Maybe, just maybe, she saw why Trey and Bailey evidently believed him. Her feeling was the kid didn't do it, however he was really not helping his situation at all, and it wasn't a good one.

She was, after all, a prosecuting attorney, but also a person and remembered being an uncertain teenager. "You are," she said reasonably, "making this very hard on yourself, and on me."

CHAPTER FIVE

It was difficult not to know how the actors were acting behind the curtain. Too much inquiry and you could give yourself away.

What do you know? That question hung there, like a ghost in the room, unseen but present.

It made life difficult and sleep almost impossible.

Yet, interestingly enough, I had no regrets.

Well, yes, maybe one.

* * *

He was really just there to sit in and listen, but what the hell.

Chris decided to ask the same question but put it differently, though maybe it was right or wrong, hard to tell. He leaned forward and asked, "So, where would you get the gun? It isn't so much what did you do with it to get rid of it, but where did it come from? If you look at it from my viewpoint, that's the big question. If your plan is to kill everyone else in the house, why not take the loaded weapons from your stepfather's dresser? Seems easier always to look at it from the killer's viewpoint. It's logical to assume you'd know they were there. Randy said you didn't have one of your own, but could get one."

For a moment Colin looked nonplussed, but then said, "I didn't plan anything. You talked to Randy?"

"Of course I did. I've talked to quite a few people who know you. The principal at your high school, all of your neighbors, your track coach from last year . . . he told me he thought you might get a college athletic scholarship easy in long distance in addition to some academic ones."

"That's not going to happen now, is it." The remark was tinged with bitterness but also resignation. There was just a slight hesitation. "Who else?"

Chris just went on because it was his strict policy to ask the questions, not answer any. "Let me think out loud. Why would you go through the trouble of getting another gun unless you are guilty? On the other hand, why would you, if you are innocent, go through the trouble of getting *rid* of the gun? The obvious answer is that you are protecting someone, though why you'd want to shield someone who killed your family is a very pressing question, don't you agree?"

If he did, he didn't say so. Just stony silence from the main suspect.

The detective in him went on reflectively. "You see, the other three people in this room besides me and yourself are very interested in whether or not you are in real trouble. I'm different. I need to know if there is a person out there who might do this again. My job is to prevent crime. If you did it, then it is over. You are caught. If you didn't, however, they might do it again. That's my concern."

Stephanie St. James gave Chris an assessing look from those noticeable dark-blue eyes before she turned back to Colin. "If you are listening to Detective Bailey at all, please realize you will have to answer tough questions like these and more, under oath, if we go to trial."

"We've discussed it." Trey Austin's tone was even. "He's very aware."

"If he'd tell us where he put the actual weapon used in the crimes, my hands would not be quite so tied." St. James wasn't giving on that point and Chris couldn't blame her.

The social worker, Ms. Hernandez, said quietly, "Please listen to her, Colin. I know Stephanie very well. What she wants is justice for those you lost, and the detective is correct, it is puzzling you don't seem to feel the same way."

"I do." He turned away, looking at once very young, his gaze unfocused.

If there was one thing Chris's job had taught him was that he was used to cornered people.

What had him so cornered was a real question.

He decided in this situation, he wasn't a good guy or a bad guy. In a calm tone, he said, "Are you protecting your biological father?"

"No!" His head lifted and his startled reaction seemed genuine. "I don't even *know* him."

"His name isn't on your birth certificate, so I believe that, and that is a matter of public record, but since you are protecting someone, he is the first logical choice. What did your mother tell you about him?"

"Nothing." He took in a deep breath. "That's nice, isn't it? She told me nothing. Just that it didn't work out. Hell, I was six when she married Joe. I just accepted what she said. Actually, I still do. I never bothered to ask again."

"But maybe it wasn't his choice to be off the grid, it was hers. Then she married someone else."

"Then he took a long while to react violently, didn't he?" Colin's blue eyes were steady. "I'm almost eighteen. I have no feelings one way or the other about him. For all I know he lives in Siberia or someplace like that."

"My take is that he should be a person of interest."

"My take is he can't possibly care what happened to my mother one way or the other."

But what if he cares about what happens to you?

That was an angle he'd tried to investigate, but had no success.

So far.

Someone retained a high-profile attorney and that was not an insignificant expense. Colin had one uncle, on his mother's side, in the US Navy. He was stationed at a foreign base currently and on sea duty. He had been contacted about the deaths of his sister and mother but he couldn't be there immediately. He'd said he would hire someone to handle the funeral details, or that was the latest word. Anna Hernandez had been forthcoming with what little she knew when he'd called.

It was a situation that left Colin completely adrift, but probably the best the man could do. Chris understood completely what it was like to be in foreign territory and at the mercy of the whims of a politically charged world while serving in the military because his brother was an officer stationed overseas. Tensions were high and your personal problems were not a priority, and you can't turn around an aircraft carrier mid-deployment for one man.

The uncle had hired no one yet, but *someone* had hired Trey Austin's firm.

Someone had also set up a trust for Colin and the trust had regularly paid child support to Roxanne Gaines through a bank officer, but either Colin didn't know that or else he was being as close-mouthed about that as he was about the gun.

Chris decided to be blunt because he leaned that direction anyway. "Do you want me to find who killed your parents and grandmother?"

That question was answered by silence, but there was a sense that Colin wanted to answer it, and he looked away, blinking quickly.

Real men don't cry, Chris got the mentality, but the truth was, occasionally they did. The show of emotion — or the struggle to hide it — was telling anyway. He said, "You don't have to answer now, but let me tell you, in court, Ms. St. James was absolutely correct, you do. Let me put it this way, if the IRS contacts an individual with a notification of an audit because a red flag has been raised about their tax return, and the defense offered is a simple declaration that they didn't cheat, but they refuse to turn over the paperwork, what is the assumption? Because if they didn't do anything wrong, why would they have to hide it, even if they are telling the truth?"

"Yeah, don't hand them the reasonable doubt, Trey has already told me that."

Obviously Austin had established some measure of trust with his young client for the natural use of his first name.

"You might consider taking his advice."

Silence again.

"Okay." After a moment Stephanie St. James stood. "You won't be present for the arraignment so Mr. Austin will be the one to inform you of all the charges brought against you if more are filed, so keep in mind you have a few days anyway to decide if you will help Detective Bailey do his job. Please think it over."

* * *

Trey walked out with the detective because there was just no way in hell he wanted to stay behind with Anna after Stephanie left. "I appreciate the time and effort your department is putting in on keeping this an open case."

Bailey was actually pretty young to be a detective, but seemed sharp and perceptive. He'd certainly handled Colin pretty well. "No problem. I'm sure you realize we aren't a large county with a lot of resources, but I can tell you the sheriff really expects us to do our jobs. He is a tough ole bird, as they say down in our neck of the woods.".

"The neck of the woods where you worked and solved a pretty significant serial case this summer? You aren't a bunch of country boys playing at law enforcement. It seems like you've overturned every rock."

"Nope, we aren't playing and I agree that I have. We're dead serious about the whole thing." He glanced over. "So who is this very nice, polite, intelligent young man willing to go to prison for?"

Trey shook his head. "Not quite yet a man. I assume you remember what it is like to be seventeen."

"Good point. I've tried hard to get a lead on a girlfriend because she might know, but it hasn't happened. He's had some in the past, because I asked the friends of his I interviewed. Just no one lately, but they do think maybe he's been seeing someone. I'm hoping Randy Price might come through for me. I sensed he knew something but didn't want to be the one to tell."

That was an interesting theory Trey hadn't considered except in passing. His car was parked by Stephanie's sleek vehicle because they'd arrived at the same time and she was sitting in her car, talking on the phone. "And keeping it a secret? Surely he's just plain too young to have had anyone so heartbroken she'd kill his parents and grandmother."

"Anything is possible. Ever had a bad break-up?"

Ouch. Trey said dryly, "Yes, now that you mention it. Ms. Hernandez, who we just left with my client, is my ex-wife."

Bailey's brows went up. "Okay, I . . . see. That accounts for the tension that I sensed in the room."

It was hell and gone more complicated than that, but he'd said enough. "For some of it, yes. We're civil, but I'm not exactly thrilled, and doubt she is either, that Colin's case belongs to her. That said, she's dedicated to her job, so he's in good hands. I can't object to that."

"And her to you?"

"I'd like to think even in her most derisive moments she would never say I'm not a capable attorney."

"Thanks for the clarification because I have to admit I was wondering about her not-quite-hidden animosity. I've been in some interesting situations because of my occupation, that's for sure. Ever lost a case?"

"That went to trial, not yet." Then Trey said with resignation, "But I don't think I've ever argued one like this when the evidence is so against my client, and it is entirely his fault because he won't cooperate. Steph is trying, and so am I, as are you, and he's hanging himself."

"I believe they don't do that any longer in this state, but we can be on the primitive side now and then here in the hills and hollers."

Trey had to appreciate the humorless cynical observation. "We *do* have the death penalty. I can't see her office going for first degree, but then again, they could. Three execution style murders. It isn't pretty to imagine."

"I saw the crime scene first hand. Not pretty at all."

"I can say honestly I would not want your job." Police officers did work the front lines. His job was more to sort out the fallout.

Bailey shrugged. "People do bad things. We catch them at it — sometimes — you make sure the law holds them accountable."

"Sometimes is the operative word. The system works, and sometimes it does not. In this case, I hope it does. I can't discuss what my clients tell me, but I can say to you that on a personal level I believe what he has told law enforcement."

He also thought from this interview today Stephanie did too, so that was a step in the right direction.

"I might have a slant on this that is unusual, but until I look into it, I'm just guessing, and we don't get to draw conclusions as detectives. If anything comes of it, I'll let you know."

"Fair enough. I appreciate it."

He watched Bailey walk away and took out his keys to press a button to unlock his car but was stopped by a feminine voice.

"Trey, hold on a minute? Did that prove worth it in your opinion? What did Detective Bailey have to say?" Stephanie was off her phone call and had gotten out of her car, her expression apologetic. "I know you're busy and have given a lot of your day already to this, but I'm really on the line and so is your client."

"He has some sort of angle in mind that he described as unusual."

He couldn't help but notice how the sunlight caught her fair hair and emphasized the indigo color of her eyes.

Yes, he definitely remembered what it was like to be seventeen and have a crush on a pretty girl.

"Good to know."

He gave her a measured look. "If Colin goes to trial for murder, they are going to move the venue in order to get an unbiased jury. This county's population is too small. You'll still prosecute, and I'll defend, but I bet your secondary counsel will be one of theirs."

"I know they'll move it. This is an emotional case for this entire state. We cooperate."

He leaned against his car and folded his arms. "What are you thinking?"

She looked away and shook her head. "Second degree probably. I don't know." Then she gave him a challenging look. "Let's turn the tables here. How would you charge him?"

"Probably that," he conceded. "You don't have enough for one, but for two, yes. Only because of the gun. You heard me in there, I'm trying to get him to see the gravity of this, and I actually think he does, but let's keep in mind he's also grieving and there's just no one to hold his hand. Is he considering this clearly? Probably not, and the only role I can assume is the one that is trying to save his ass the best I can."

At least she gave a glimmer of a smile. "Is that what is on your shingle? Attorney Trey Austin. Let Me Save Your Ass."

He laughed but smiled back. "Catchy, right?"

"I like it as a slogan."

He was almost there. Standing on the precipice of asking if, when this was done, would she have dinner with him? A date without any discussion of anything to do with their respective jobs, when she looked past him and said, "Here comes Anna. I want to talk to her."

This was clearly not the right time. "I don't. I'm out of here."

CHAPTER SIX

Their deaths solved nothing.

I'm still angry and that is an ongoing theme anyway, but the problem itself remains.

If I were a different person I would have dealt with this in another way, I know it.

History just repeats itself, right?

I worry about that.

* * *

Nice day, a little cool, but the air smelled like fall, fresh and clean.

Anna glanced at Stephanie who had walked across the parking lot to meet her. "What did you take away from that little meeting?"

Her friend looked thoughtful, her brow furrowed, hair shining in the afternoon sun. "I'm still processing. Were you told exactly why Detective Bailey was there?"

Anna wasn't quite sure how to respond, moodily watching Trey's expensive car pull away. "I would think you'd know more about that than I do. He did call me and asked me a few questions. I'm not sure why exactly, since he seemed to know everything anyway."

"He's a detective with a small department, but he has a much more impressive resume than what appears on the surface."

"And that means . . . what?"

"He solved, as far as I can tell, three different cases all at once last summer, all homicides tied to various locations." Stephanie shook her head. "A rather incredible set of circumstances, but he seems to be adept in cases that are complicated. Like Colin's."

"And you know this how?"

"I've stayed at his cabin in the woods. We spent a memorable night together."

That stopped her cold. "Excuse me? You, me and Trey interacting on a professional basis was awkward enough. Detective Bailey didn't even factor into that statement. Care to clarify?"

"I slept in the same room with his little dog, not him, in case you are wondering."

"I might have been," Anna admitted. "How did you end up in that situation?"

"I had a problem and was stuck on a country road one night and he came along and played knight in shining armor. He was off duty, and waiting until morning seemed the best solution. He was headed to this little cabin he has on the river and so we went there."

No hardship on his part, Anna was sure enough of that. Attractive blonde in distress late at night, why not carry her off to a remote cabin. For that matter, Detective Bailey was a good-looking guy so he would make an ideal hero, though being in the same room as Trey made for some tough competition for any male.

Get over it. It was a silent plea she made to herself every single time she saw her ex-husband.

The divorce had been the right decision, that wasn't the regret. You can't lose something you never actually had in the first place, or so she reminded herself all too often. However, you *can* lose an optimistic view of romantic love.

Hers had been left behind in the dust, the chances of finding it again not very high.

"Nice of him." Anna reached her car and stopped. Stephanie's vehicle was a few spots down. She squared her shoulders. "Will you clue me in on what might be going on? I can talk to Trey, but I'm sure you aren't surprised I'd like to keep that as minimal as possible. We speak, but it is painful politeness at best."

Stephanie stopped as well, the light breeze ruffling her fair hair, her expression very hard to read. "You've never said exactly what caused the split, but it seemed — from the outside looking in anyway — to be not contentious."

It was impossible to stifle a humorless laugh. "Good, we pulled that act off anyway. As far as I can tell, there is no such thing as a truly amicable divorce, but speaking from experience, for a lawyer, Trey does not like to argue. You know full well I speak my mind."

"That's why I've been surprised you've never explained, not that it is really my business, but usually you talk to me."

That was true. *Close friends since childhood, same high school, same activities, college roommates, maid of honor at my ill-fated wedding . . .*

Not her business, Stephanie was wrong there.

"I'm doing my best to just set it aside and go forward."

"I understand."

No, she didn't. Maybe someday they'd *have* to have a discussion, but for now, Anna just wasn't ready.

So she changed the subject back. "Keep me informed about the case, please?"

Stephanie let it go, but she would, she was sensitive like that. "Like I explained, Colin won't be there for the arraignment. I will let you know how it is decided. Unfortunately, Detective Bailey had one very good point that I'd certainly already considered, but maybe Colin needed to hear it. It can be argued if he chose to go looking for a weapon instead of using his stepfather's, he premediated those three deaths. He also was right about getting rid of the weapon. It just plain makes him look guilty, especially with the eyewitness. I am supposed to get full disclosure from Trey on evidence, of course, but he doesn't have to tell me how he might argue his case. What he needs is to offer up someone else with the same opportunity. The court cares about motive only if it is very compelling. I don't think Colin has one we can see, but plenty of opportunity."

"From what I understand there was no sign someone broke in." It was troubling.

"Correct. Whoever committed the murders either used a key, or the Gaines's house was unlocked. Colin claims he doesn't know whether or not the door was actually locked. He can't remember hearing a click when he used his key, but reasonably so, wasn't paying a lot of attention. At that time, he didn't know anything was wrong. *If* he didn't do it."

"Just the same, it doesn't look good, does it?" Anna sighed and said with heartfelt conviction, "I'm glad I'm not in your shoes. I know this isn't your first homicide case, but I also know you haven't had one like this."

"I'm happy to say it isn't the norm, that's for sure. Even my boss doesn't have much in the way of advice on how to handle it. They were right to bump it up from juvenile court and my real problem is that I believe the accused, but is it just because I want to?"

"I want to as well. If I had to guess, so does Trey."

"He and I have only been opposing counsel in one significant case so far." Stephanie looked resigned. "I don't have to tell you he's a talented lawyer. He never presents an unprepared witness for testimony, and he doesn't make mistakes by assuming anything. I really don't have much choice but to charge him because Colin is making it impossible for me to do otherwise. I feel sorry for both Trey and myself. I have to pursue this case and he has to defend his client, and both of us want it to turn out Colin is not the one who did it, but I bet I'm going to win, unless Bailey does what the defense hopes he will do."

"Someone else with opportunity and motive?"

Stephanie nodded and said with wry emphasis, "All he needs to do is solve the crime. No pressure." She paused and added, "I'm not joking. At this point, I think he's the only card we have to play on either side."

Anna had to agree. "Colin has no idea who retained Trey for him. That's certainly another interesting part of this problem that has been dumped in my lap. I'd love to find an individual who could take legal custody of him until he's of age and I'm sure his uncle would, but he's not in the country. I have been able to exchange emails, but the difference in time zones makes it difficult, and he's on duty pretty much all the time as far as I can tell, plus he doesn't quite know what to do either at this point. When Colin is charged in court, there might still be no point in him pulling all the strings necessary to get back to the States, because Colin will be held unless he makes bail, if it is offered at all, and I'm going to guess it will be high."

"Yes." Steph didn't equivocate.

"I don't how much a naval officer makes, but I doubt it is enough to have the resources to scrounge it up. I know he's concerned, but I don't get the impression that he even knows Colin all that well. He's an older brother and unmarried. He has a house, but it is near Virginia Beach where we have a big naval base. So just an occasional visit here to see his mother and sister."

And now he had neither. Just a nephew involved with their murders.

Quite frankly, she wouldn't blame him for just not doing anything and letting the courts handle it.

"I'm going to talk to the district attorney this afternoon." Stephanie sounded resigned. "He is old-school, Anna. But I will say he doesn't like to bring charges if he's doubtful we are going to win. I don't know what he will advise me to do, and I don't have to take his advice but there will be second counsel on this if we go to trial as well. The D.A. is the voice of experience. We'll see. It isn't just me."

Fair enough.

Anna took a breath and made a decision. "Let's have dinner soon? No talk of this case, just two friends catching up?"

Stephanie looked understandably surprised because Anna hadn't been open to social interaction for quite some time. "Well . . . absolutely."

"Look at your schedule and send me a text? I have to run."

A first step, she thought as she walked away.

Her therapist would approve.

* * *

Stressful day that never got better.

Stephanie toed off her shoes and looked at the number on her phone to see a call she declined to answer. It was definitely time for a glass of wine.

She chose a nice Merlot, opened the bottle, and went to pour a glass. Good vintage, nice and smooth with a velvet touch of blackberry overtones and a hint of brandy . . .

What the hell did Daniel want?

He was two years gone from her life. There was no doubt she'd known he was a mistake all along. Too self-absorbed, undeniably charismatic, a sexy smile, but following his own way without regard for anyone else.

He hadn't taken her decision to walk away well. His unhidden anger had resulted in an unpleasant scene that had left her shaken and more convinced than ever she'd made the right choice. If it hadn't been for her occupation, she was convinced it would have gotten physical. As it was, she immediately had her locks changed and even considered a restraining order.

It revealed a part of him she'd sensed might be there but had never seen in action before.

He'd left a message.

I still think about you all the time.

There was no doubt it took some restraint to not answer back: *No, you think about you all the time.*

She didn't. Just deleted it.

The interaction with Anna had been interesting. She'd not taken the split with Trey well at all, and yet it was her decision. That there was some measure of angst as a residue of it might be expected.

Yet Stephanie had been shut out too.

There was a worry she knew the reason.

The knock on her door startled her. No visitors expected.

So much for no shoes and a lonesome glass of wine, she thought with a twinge of curiosity as she went to the door, taking a cautious look before she opened it. Gray hair pulled back in a tidy bun, a cardigan over a white shirt, navy Capri pants, red tennis shoes, the usual uniform. Stephanie was surprised. "Hello Mrs. Burke."

Her next-door neighbor was a nice lady, widowed and mid-sixties, who religiously took a walk each day, put out hummingbird feeders in the summer and fed the squirrels in the winter, and tended a small garden behind her condo so Stephanie was occasionally gifted with tomatoes, which she appreciated.

The older woman eyed her wine glass. "Stephanie. I'm not interrupting anything, I hope."

"No. Just a long day at work. Uhm, come in?"

It just seemed like her neighbor had something to say. "I won't stay long. I just have a concern and decided you being who you are, I should say something."

Since she didn't sense overt disapproval over the alcohol consumption, Stephanie stepped back in invitation. "If I can help, of course I will. I just opened a bottle, would you like a glass of wine?"

"That would be nice, actually. I don't often, but now and then I indulge."

"Please have a seat and I'll go get a glass." She motioned at the couch, glad she'd dusted recently, and other than her shoes on the floor, the living room was tidy. In general, she liked an ordered life, and she wasn't home really all that much, so generally her condo was well-kept, but occasionally she left dishes in the sink or the laundry piled up.

As she took a glass from the cupboard and poured the wine, she wondered what sort of legal advice Mrs. Burke could possibly need. Naturally people did ask now and then. Her sister's husband was a financial advisor and she certainly picked his brain whenever she was going to make a major monetary decision and that was how the world worked.

She went back into the living room, handed over the wine and sat down in an armchair by the window and politely waited.

Her guest took a sip, and raised her brows appreciatively. Then she said briskly, "Actually, I'm here to possibly help you, honey. I don't know a lot about this sort of thing, and I'd like to think I'm not a busybody or nosy person or however you'd term it, but I think you have a stalker."

Whatever she expected to hear, that wasn't it. And it was unwelcome after that unexpected call from Daniel.

After a moment, she said cautiously, "Can you clarify for me why you came to this conclusion?"

"Spoken like a true lawyer." Patricia Burke said the words with underlying humor but then explained succinctly, "There is a woman that I do not recognize as belonging to this neighborhood that seems to be keeping an eye on your arrivals and departures for the past few days or so. There is no doubt in my mind she is watching you. Sometimes she just sits in her car, sometimes she just walks by, and this morning, after you left, she went up to your front door and looked in the glass side panel."

Well, not Daniel anyway.

Considering her neighbor made the rounds each day on her walks, Stephanie believed her that there was someone out of the ordinary around. "Can you describe her?"

"Better yet. I took a picture with my phone. Take a look."

She accepted the phone and shook her head at the image on the screen. Maybe fortyish, dark hair, medium build; it was a decent enough picture. "I don't know her."

"With your occupation, honey, I always worry about you making an unknown enemy."

"I appreciate your concern, so thank you. Can you send this picture to me? That way, now that I'm aware, if I see someone I can compare."

"I'd be glad to, and rest assured I'm now keeping an eye out. How is the case going?"

There was no doubt it had gotten a lot of press. She was not allowed to discuss anything pending, so she just said neutrally, "As well as any case like this can go."

"Very tragic, I agree. Why would any young man kill off his family?"

The entire problem was Stephanie just didn't think he had. "I'm not a psychologist."

"I'm not either, but this woman is very interested in you for some reason and it came about right after he was taken in by the police."

CHAPTER SEVEN

The sound of voices resonates in an unkind way.
   The ones in my head are worse than those around me.
   This had better go the way I want it to.
   Otherwise I worry what might happen next.
   The nurse came out and called my first name.
   I went.

* * *

"Do you mind giving me a clue as to what you are doing?"

Chris glanced up from frowning at his computer as his partner came up, shirt and tie perfectly in place as always. In contrast, he was in his usual jeans and what barely passed for a decently pressed denim shirt, his sidearm always visible in the shoulder holster since he never wore a jacket.

"Clarify?" He leaned back in his chair.

"You requested an appointment for both of us with a senator from the great state of Tennessee through the sheriff's office in Washington, D.C.?"

"Oh yeah, I did."

"It is your turn now." Carter sat down in the one chair by Chris's desk and rubbed his forehead. "Clarify, and why do I have a feeling I don't want to hear this?"

"I need to know what is going on with this case."

"And Senator Grayson can tell you? I'm dying to know how you can make this connection."

"Maybe he can."

"Why?"

"I really can't tell you how I came by this information."

It had taken considerable persuasion to get the person who revealed the information after he finally tracked them down. He would keep his word he would never mention their name.

"Bailey, anything that isn't done strictly by the book is not admissible in court."

Chris straightened and lifted his hands. "Hey, I didn't do anything. It came to me by a strict promise of anonymity. But it is an intriguing lead, I admit it. If it is true, it solves a few problems but probably creates some as well."

"Okay, that sounds about usual when it comes to you. Tell me."

"The senator is related to our as-of-yet not charged suspect in a triple homicide."

"Oh shit. Father?"

Chris had to admit he blinked. Carter did not use profanity.

"I'd guess. Colin's mother is dead so we can't ask her, but we *can* ask him. Seventeen years ago she did work for his office and he was married, but only forty-one years old. Already in public service, so that might be why his name is not on the birth certificate and she was paid quiet child support."

Carter looked away and shook his head. "Which is why the kid has Austin as an attorney. You do realize both of us have to keep this to ourselves. Oh man, every morning I get up and hope a freight train is not going to run over me and quite frequently I am disappointed and get flattened on the rails. Fine, I guess an interview is in order, but I bet we'll have to wear sunglasses and meet in a crowded trendy bistro or something. I am too old for this subversive intrigue."

"I highly doubt either one of us is sophisticated enough to navigate anything subversive, so let's just see how his office responds. My accent alone would let them know I'm from right down here. But so is he. He does represent our state. I'm kinda hoping he'll just come home for a brief meeting."

"You think he'll come back to Tennessee from Washington to meet with a couple of detectives from this county for a few questions?" Carter looked skeptical.

"I'm thinking he will because he might decide we would mess up the covert meeting thing in D.C. Like we will wear cowboy boots and say ya'll and carry unconcealed weapons."

Carter didn't have much of a sense of humor most of the time, but he did laugh. "That would be you."

"Guilty as charged." He paused. "You know, he's evidently concerned about his son enough to retain an attorney that will do his best to protect him."

"*If* your theory is correct."

"Only he can tell me at this point. I can tell you that Colin doesn't know."

"Who his father is?"

"According to him, no."

"If the kid is innocent, I feel for him."

"Me too. He is really alone."

"Maybe not. We'll just play it your way."

His phone rang then, and Chris looked at the name and number and had to admit the timing was pretty damn good. "Don't leave quite yet. Let's find out what the man has to say."

* * *

Trey didn't break for lunch very often. Usually it was a sandwich at his desk, but on occasion he'd make an exception.

Today was one of those days.

Bailey was there, sitting at a table in the corner studying his phone screen, but he glanced up with instant awareness when he walked in the door.

The man was a detective and a law enforcement officer. Nothing about this was likely to be good news.

"Austin. Thanks for meeting me."

Trey took a seat opposite, and the waitress immediately brought him a menu. Good, they were both busy men. "Of course, if it pertains to my client's case."

"It does. The burger is decent here but I prefer the Rueben."

If there was one thing he was learning about Bailey, it was that he rarely approached anything head-on but circled around. "That sounds fine." He handed back the menu. The waitress was young and pretty but wasn't Stephanie so it didn't matter that she gave him a flirtatious smile.

His smile back was just polite and he turned back to his companion. No need to get her interested in a lost cause, because he sure as hell was one.

He needed to get over feeling sorry for himself.

If this was a fairy tale, he'd be the one who did not win the fair maiden.

"So why are we here?"

"I think I found your client's father so this is a courtesy in case he holds you accountable, because I assume he's the one who has taken on the task of paying you to help his son."

Well hell.

No, not good news.

"I do not disclose."

"If only you had I wouldn't have had to work so hard to figure it out."

"Detective Bailey, I can't break confidentiality."

"I understand that, so that's why you are here. I talked to him and made it clear you were not the source of my information."

That was something anyway.

"Was he able to help with the investigation?"

"Well, I think knowing his identity and that he seems to have a solid alibi takes him off the suspect list. People keep track of U.S. senators."

So Detective Bailey really had figured it out. Trey just shook his head, unwilling to confirm or deny. "I feel confident that what my client told you in our interview was the truth. He knows nothing about his biological father."

"I feel confident *I* know why. He was a married man who had an affair and wanted to avoid the political embarrassment, not to mention possibly the financial and personal ramifications of how it would affect his marriage." It seemed like Bailey was more musing aloud than anything. "I do admire his sense of responsibility that he was willing to make financial commitments to his child's future, but there's an even greater cost. I can't imagine having a kid I couldn't talk to, or who didn't even know my name. That's just my take on this situation."

Silently, Trey agreed. He wanted a family and he knew Anna had as well, but truth be told, it was just as well she hadn't gotten pregnant because a broken relationship made for a very different kind of parenting than what he would want for his children. Stable life, two loving parents being part of the day to day had been his childhood and he was lucky compared to some of his friends as he grew up.

Look at Colin. No idea of who his father was, but if there were any complaints about Joe Gaines, he hadn't voiced them.

"My impression is Colin liked his stepfather well enough."

"According to the people I talked to at the school, the man attended all his track meets and even went so far to help out selling concessions and taking tickets. A good guy — or that was their take on it."

"Tell me how you think this will assist the investigation, for I certainly have a vested interest in you being able to solve this crime and point a finger in another direction."

"It was a personal crime." Bailey looked reflective. "My take on it is that whoever went into that house with ill-intent was not an average killer and there's an agenda going in this case. Revenge? Envy? Gain? The question is for what? Or who was the target? The political slant on it bothers me."

58

Their lunch arrived and put a pause to the conversation, but Trey had to admit those were all good questions. He'd really not considered this could be aimed at the senator.

"Do you two want anything to drink besides water?"

He didn't usually at this time of day, but Trey said, "I'll take a beer, thank you."

Bailey clearly approved. "Make it two."

The sandwich was really good as promised, the beer nice and cold, but he was distracted by an inner contemplation — had he been looking at this incorrectly? If the only way to protect his client was to drag out his father's career path, then his hands were tied. There was a clear request for total silence. It wasn't just an ethical question. He couldn't do it.

Trey finally said, "I agree, it was a personal crime, and ruthless. Now I'm worried if someone else found out — you did — and is getting some payback by framing his innocent young son."

"And we are both sitting here wondering who would hate him that much."

"With neither one of us in a position to really find out. From down here, I am not necessarily connected to politics, state or federal."

"Yes we are. In Washington is where they create the law. You practice it and I enforce it."

He took a drink of his beer. "Okay, so what is it you want, because while I don't dabble my toes in the nuances of policy and so forth, you want something from me. That I recognize."

"Talk to him and just ask that simple question. You want to help his son and he does too obviously so both of you help me. I want to take someone off the streets that committed cold-blooded murder. Three people are dead. I don't think I'm asking too much of either of you. There's a connection we are missing. Is it him? I don't know. I can't really talk to him because he will never admit to the affair to a public servant, but you can."

"No disclosure."

"Exactly."

"So this lunch is to get me to give you disclosure that I can't give."

"No, to get him to allow you to just talk to me about what Colin tells you. The kid seems to like you."

"At this point, Anna has to consent, and in case you didn't notice, we are no longer close friends."

"So ask him to ask her. It means he'll have to tell her who he is but just as you are ethically bound to keep confidentiality, she surely is bound by similar rules when it comes to her charges. I personally think she should know anyway. She's making decisions for his child."

"I am not saying one way or the other if the senator is even involved in this."

Bailey shook his head, laughing. "Give me one reason for a DNA swab and this conversation is over."

Trey was a lawyer. "Your problem is you need that reason."

"Yeah. I know. I need you to let me do my job. I want to help your client, because my gut, which has been pretty reliable in the past, says he didn't do it."

They were on the same page.

"But you think he knows who did."

"That isn't clear to me, but he's a pretty smart kid from all accounts."

Trey considered him across the table. "I think he suspects."

"So you'll talk to him?"

He nodded. "That's a good way to go about it."

When he left the nice waitress had a good tip and Chris Bailey had a U.S. senator in his pocket, though luckily, Trey was fairly sure he had no agenda.

He was a true lawman.

There were not enough of them but they apparently still did exist.

Maybe he didn't sport a badge, but Trey thought he was one as well, wanting justice, and to protect potential future victims.

Not a bad partnership in his opinion.

He called Stephanie on his way back to the office. "I just met with Bailey, and—"

"I'm actually at your office. Do you have a time of arrival? I have a full day but hoped you'd be in. It is hardly a big deal, but maybe we need to talk."

CHAPTER EIGHT

It isn't as if this served any purpose.

I question my motives more than anyone else at times.

Sometimes they are crystal clear to me, like gazing at the bottom of a running stream, water bubbling over the pebbles.

At others the flow is muddy and sluggish, hard to see through it, and I simply drift with the current.

So I drove by the empty house and wondered why I bothered.

* * *

Stephanie sat in a leather chair and philosophically contemplated the difference between her very functional work space as an attorney employed by the public sector, and Trey's extremely posh corner office. It had a view and a private bathroom as he was a top lawyer with a firm that literally represented clients from across the country, the more high profile the better.

It was hard to say who had the harder job. He just made more money defending than she did prosecuting.

The purpose of this impromptu visit might just be a waste of time, but the truth was, she needed to talk to someone and Trey seemed a natural choice. They worked on the opposite side of the equation, but they were colleagues, had known each other for quite some time, and he was unequivocally one of the most intelligent men she knew.

He was true to his promise and was only ten minutes away. That was about all she could spare.

"Steph?" He came in and set down a briefcase by his desk, a sharply inquiring look in his eyes. "What's up? I wanted to talk to you and you obviously want to talk to me so this works out. Feel free to go first."

"I'm not sure my question has anything to do with the Simon case. You go first and tell me what Detective Bailey had to say. Then we'll address my concern."

"That's the strategy? Force me to be the offense?" He looked amused and his flashing smile was the one she wondered if any woman could ever resist. The truth was, she knew for a fact it worked on just about any female within his range.

It did on her.

With composure, she responded, "What you have to say certainly pertains to the case we are mutually working on, and what I have to say may not."

He sat down behind his polished desk, and nodded. "Okay, fair enough. Bailey seems to be able to pick up a scent without any trouble and he has an interesting lead on this case I can't quite dismiss out of hand. As defense counsel I am supposed to tell you if other individuals will be deposed, and there might be an interesting one depending on how he decides to handle this. I can't really stop him. What would be nice is if we could all just work together toward our common goal which is catching who really killed three people, but we are not allowed to do that."

"Is this the person who is paying you for his defense?"

"No comment." He arched his dark brows. "Your turn."

It was why she was there anyway. Stephanie took out her phone. "There's a woman who seems very interested in me, and by all accounts, it started after Colin was taken into custody. Do you recognize her?"

"Interested in you? How?" He looked at the screen and shook his head. "And no, I don't have any idea who she is."

"She's apparently watching my house and paying attention to when I come and go. My neighbor noticed and took that picture."

"That makes me uneasy."

"I wasn't happy to hear it either, and I have seen her since. Outside my office this morning."

He stared at her with those compelling dark eyes and leaned back in his chair. "Steph, really?"

"Do you think it can be related to the fact I'm handling this case?"

It took a moment but he said quietly, "I don't see how, but who can say. You have other cases."

That was true enough. "This one is high profile."

"Oh, don't I know it. A camp divided out there. You are prosecuting a kid that lost his family if you're wrong, and I'm defending a murderer if I'm wrong."

"We don't get to decide if a person is guilty or not, we just present the evidence one way or the other."

"I'm well aware."

His ironic tone made her give a short laugh. "I know. I'm just trying to look for some guidance on how to handle this stalker, if she is one. Ignore it or walk over and confront her and ask what she wants. Thoughts?"

"Steph, you're beautiful."

That was a nice compliment but what it had to do with what they were talking about was a mystery. "First of all, thanks, and care to explain how that — if it is even true — pertains to this conversation because I'm not following your thread."

He spread his hands. "If someone was jealous of you, it would not surprise me. I'm thinking like a lawyer and trying to be analytical here. In the Simon case, why would anyone involved be interested in your life enough to shadow you?"

He had a point, which was exactly why she wanted to talk to him. She sighed. "Please tell me it has nothing to do with Daniel."

That certainly caught his interest. "Why would it? You two went your separate ways quite a while ago."

"Yes. But he texted me just last night. Why would he?"

"I have an ex-wife who is bitter for reasons that are still unclear to me. Please don't ask me to explain failed relationships."

He had a point. She'd never understood either why Anna had ever filed for divorce.

If he thought she was beautiful, he hadn't looked in the mirror. He was a very good-looking man, plain and simple, if you liked the cliché of tall, dark and handsome. But his looks aside, he was also even-tempered as far as she knew, reasonable, unquestionably intelligent and had a sense of humor.

Slowly he said, "I suppose if he has a girlfriend and she knows about you and that he's contacted you, she could be jealous, or at least wondering if he has lingering doubts about whether it is over or not."

"I have no idea if he is involved with anyone, and if he is, why she would care about me is a question I can't answer because it *is* over."

"It is possible she is extremely insecure he texted you, or is still interested in you. Behind the scenes is always a mystery."

"I don't know. Daniel is very interested in Daniel," she said wryly. "And let the record show, I am certainly no longer interested in him. In fact, he now disturbs me more than a little. Our split wasn't exactly amicable."

Trey's interest sharpened. "What the hell did he do?"

"Without going into detail, let's say I had a moment or two where I was actually afraid for my personal safety."

"Are you serious?"

"Let's forget about him. Give me your opinion on how to handle this."

"I'll try to remain a neutral party. He'd better not be the cause of this situation and I admit the timing is interesting. As for this woman, I'm uncomfortable with the idea of you confronting her. If she is dangerous for some reason, that just

65

seems like it might accelerate the problem. However, if your neighbor has seen her multiple times and you've now seen her near your office . . . I'm concerned."

Stephanie had considered going to stay with Lara, but with two toddlers — no. What if the woman was truly dangerous?

She considered Trey across his desk, assessed his nice wide shoulders, and lifted a brow. "Care to come over for dinner tonight? Maybe if she thinks I'm seeing someone, she might back off."

Dream come true.

Had *she* just asked *him*? Problem solved.

"Absolutely. I'll bring wine." Trey certainly hoped he pulled off an expression that didn't indicate the depth of his enthusiasm.

"Considering everything going on, wine sounds like a good idea." She paused. "Though not always. I have to ask you, has Detective Bailey said anything about how we met?"

He hadn't. "No. I assume because of the workings of our judicial system."

"It depends on how you look at it, so yes and no." She stood, as professional as ever in a skirt and blouse, long slender legs, and that elegant swing of blonde hair he always admired. "Seven o'clock?"

"You're not going to explain that cryptic statement?"

"No. So we have a date?"

"We do."

"I'll see you then."

He watched her leave and felt both a sense of gratitude and also unease over this mysterious woman. That Stephanie was being followed, or observed, or whatever you wished to call it, bothered him. Then again, it had worked out in his favor.

The rest of his afternoon was consumed with writing summaries and he had a hearing at four o'clock that was more a formality than anything else. He had to admit he put off calling the senator's office to see if they could discuss

Bailey's deductive powers but he did think the man would cooperate as much as possible if the press was left out of it. How unhappy he was that a detective from a small county had figured out Colin's parentage was probably not in question, but then again, maybe he could shed some light on a possible alternative suspect if he looked at it from the slant he might be the target.

Trey was pondering it as he went home to change out of his office clothes, choosing khakis and discarding the dress shirt and tie for a casual golf shirt. Then he perused his liquor cabinet selection with absolutely no idea what Stephanie had in mind for dinner, so selecting a Merlot and a Chardonnay to try and hopefully pair the food with the wine seemed a reasonable decision.

Then he called Bailey. He wasn't positive it was a good idea, but he'd been hired to defend Colin on what could prove to be charges that would bury his client, and this was not disclosure, this was one professional talking to another.

One ring. "Counselor?"

"Have you thought about the senator's wife?"

A small silence. "So you're favoring revenge for the motive."

"I'm not favoring anything, this is your area of expertise, but I suppose if a woman discovered her husband had fathered a love child — which is your theory — she might seek to get retribution by killing the party that wronged her and implicating her husband's son in a very heinous crime."

"Murder for hire?"

"I doubt she'd do it herself."

"Interesting theory. It would complicate things for me, but when more people are involved, mistakes are made. That might just be a direction I should look, but it means I really need to talk to folks and it will draw attention. If she doesn't know about Colin, there'd be a flaming red flag in front of her. In other words, the senator really needs to talk to me first, or he might just get himself into a raft floating down Shit River."

There was no way he could stifle a laugh. Bailey was a country boy with a badge, but he was astute and razor sharp as far as he could tell, and his record proved it.

"I'm not going to comment on that either way. This is very much on my mind. If someone tried to get at his biological father through Colin because they knew of an affair, wouldn't either blackmail or just giving the press the information make more sense if it is motivated politically? I'm sure he has those that dislike him in his line of work because we all do, but still three execution style murders is a drastic road to travel."

"Austin, you are such an attorney talking around what we both know is the truth, but I do get it, and I appreciate the nudge to seriously consider that line of inquiry. It is a real possibility."

He glanced up at the antique clock on the mantel he'd inherited from his grandmother. "I'll be interested to hear how the investigation goes forward. For now, I have a dinner date with a very lovely district attorney . . . speaking of which, how did you meet Stephanie anyway?"

"You are going to have to ask her. I'm starting to think maybe it was because of you."

What the hell did that mean?

"Your answer is just as interesting as her question to me was when she asked if you'd mentioned it."

"Enjoy your evening."

The call ended and Trey had to shake his head and then gathered up the bottles of wine and headed for the garage.

There was no way he wanted to be late for this invitation.

* * *

Chris sat at the dining-room table watching a rerun of *Star Trek* — the original version of the series — but not paying attention really.

Life did hold irony, he would never deny that.

That he'd encounter the prosecutor of the same case he was working on a lonely stretch of county highway was quite the coincidence, but that she'd be tied to the defense attorney and then factor in the social worker was his ex-wife . . .

It was stretching it, but that was somehow how it worked out with fate sitting there in the background just laughing.

However, maybe Austin had a decent angle on this complicated investigation.

The senator's wife was a true consideration, but he'd bet she had a solid alibi either way. If she had orchestrated the murders, she'd make sure of it. If she had nothing to do with it, he'd still bet their social schedule would provide one.

His trouble was how to even investigate anything like this. He was, essentially, a county cop. He didn't live in Washington, D.C., he had no connections except that the local pizza place knew exactly what he wanted when he texted in an order for delivery.

That wasn't exactly true — it occurred to him as he watched Spock dissect a problem on screen in a very logical manner. He did know a federal agent at the Nashville office of the FBI. Wright had been in on the last murder case he'd handled. She was the one who suggested he apply for a job with the bureau and though it had been a few months since they'd last talked, maybe she'd give him some insight.

He'd have to really think over how he presented it though. If this was a viable lead, it would be a big deal, and probably the FBI would get involved because of a triple homicide and a U.S. senator.

"What do you think?" he asked the moppet.

She was napping at his feet, but looked up and thought it over, tilting her head.

Her soulful eyes said she thought he should really have at least some viable evidence before he made a move in that direction.

CHAPTER NINE

The interesting relationships between parents and children have ruled the centuries. It continues and I suppose there is no end in sight.

The dynamic is fraught with the inevitable conflict of the transfer of power and a resistance to relinquish it.

One side will inevitably lose the battle.

I'm learning that the hard way.

* * *

Trey arrived as promised, two bottles of wine in hand, and Stephanie was busy making a salad. This dinner was hardly planned, so other than setting the table and checking the downstairs guest bathroom, she'd not done much other than put the chicken in the oven, prepare the potatoes, and change her clothes.

Her grandmother's recipe for French chicken. Roasted potatoes to go along — it was sworn to be the recipe to win any man's heart.

Was that what she wanted?

Maybe, but it was hardly that simple. She'd answered the knock on the door with some trepidation. "Hi."

There was a hint of humor in his reply. His mouth curved into an amused smile. "Hi."

She had to admit that it was reminiscent of a high school date and laughed. "Come on in. Anyone bearing wine is welcome."

He set the bottles on the counter when she led him into her kitchen and glanced around at the white cabinets, the butcher block counters and the polished original wood floor. "Very nice."

"Older house, so I had it redone to match the farmhouse style. Let me get two glasses."

Yes, they were both going up against each other in a case she suspected would be really complicated and tense on both sides but, she wanted, if nothing else, something from him she had no idea how to ask for, and when she found the nerve, she might do it.

No, *if* she found the nerve.

Separate the personal from the professional?

Surely possible.

Worth a try.

In shirt and tie he was a lawyer, but in casual attire he was a man with wavy dark hair, classic chiseled features, irresistible dark eyes, and an engaging smile. The professional was compelling in court and serious as hell about his job, which was why he was just so damned good at it.

She still wasn't sure she'd win their upcoming battle. She had more convincing evidence, but then again, there was a chance he could rip it apart in some way she didn't see coming

When he'd graduated he worked briefly for the public defender's office and was so effective law firms had recruited him immediately, and she wasn't surprised.

This was different.

Just the two of them. A simple dinner.

They could discuss a potential stalker and a triple murder.

Or maybe something else.

"It smells fantastic in here."

She handed him the corkscrew. "Family recipe."

"A home cooked meal is a rarity for me."

For her too. She didn't bother very often. "I don't eat out much but having a sandwich for dinner isn't unusual. I get home and I'm tired and it's just me."

"I can relate. I go over to see my parents every couple of weeks in Lynchburg and my mother makes dinner, but otherwise, like you, I just do something simple."

She'd known him quite a while, but one-on-one small talk was hardly usual between them. Either they were in professional settings, or at social gatherings and never alone in her kitchen, just the two of them.

He deftly uncorked the Chardonnay and poured two glasses.

"Let's go into the living room," she suggested. "We have about a half an hour before dinner is ready."

It was a chilly fall evening. She'd turned on the fireplace earlier so the setting was cozy and the rain had started just as predicted. The ambiance was nice with a gentle patter against the windows and the flickering flame. He settled on the couch and she took a comfortable armchair just opposite and asked, "Did you see anyone sitting in their car outside?"

"I did. Parked about two houses down on the street. I wanted to note the license plate but you know what? It is covered by what looks like a temporary paper plate that looks official enough to pass for legal."

It was exactly the time to try the wine, which proved to be quite smooth and delicious. Stephanie looked at him. "Are you serious?"

"Yeah, I am," he said it with quiet concern. "So I pulled into your driveway and whoever it was drove off. I'm glad I'm here."

"I just don't see why anyone would be the least interested in me."

"I do." The faint attractive smile that touched his mouth faded. "But that is from a purely male perspective. A strange

72

woman sitting in her car watching your house is troubling. I'm pretty good with faces and she resembled the picture you showed me, though I didn't really have a clear line of vision."

"I don't have the slightest idea who she could be."

"The problem is you can't prove she's even interested in you specifically and she hasn't threatened or harassed you, so I guess just being aware is the only option now. There is no law against just watching unless you are peering in a window."

"I know." She took another sip of wine. "If she does that again, because according to my neighbor she has but I wasn't home at the time, trust me I will report it."

"So she's trespassed?"

"There's only one eyewitness account. Hard to prove, agreed? Walked up to my front door and looked in the side glass panel. That's not against the law."

"Agreed. But sometimes it can be argued the sum of the parts could constitute a restraining order."

"Except against whom? I have no idea of her identity. And they really don't do much more than make the person aware you perceive them as a threat."

Part of the reason she hadn't done it with Daniel. She didn't want him to know he'd frightened her.

"If they are concealing their identity by using a fake license plate, watching your house, following you to work, and looking in a window, you could make a valid argument for stalking."

"Only if I had the slightest clue who she is and what she wants."

His smile was rueful. "Okay, you win there. Maybe ask Bailey to look into it, except I think his hands are pretty full. I called him just before I came here with a theory, if I can even put it that way, of someone who might have been responsible for the homicides besides Colin."

He wouldn't tell her who, she already knew better than to ask. They were, after all, on a different side on this and that would be a serious lapse. "Was he interested?"

"He didn't just hear me politely, I believe he listened." There was a pause and his gaze was inquiring. "I asked him how you two met, since you asked me if he'd said anything, and he told me I'd have to ask you. So?"

* * *

Stephanie had changed into faded jeans that hugged her hips and long legs and a long-sleeved feminine shirt in a soft rose color. It was just as casual as it should be for the setting and the impromptu invitation, but somehow managed to be as eye-catching as anything she wore, which probably meant the woman inside of it was the key denominator.

She obviously considered her answer. "We met under unusual circumstances and spent the night together at his picturesque cabin."

That wasn't the answer he expected — or wanted. "I see."

He had no right to react with any kind of stab of jealousy.

But it happened anyway.

"I slept in the same bed with his little dog, not with him," she expounded. "He was nice about the whole thing."

Nice about what?

He waited but apparently no further explanation was forthcoming.

Fair enough. What she'd just said was a relief.

Instead she murmured, "The wine is really nice. Good choice."

And left him wondering how on earth she could have spent the night with a detective because of him. That enigmatic comment needed explaining, but for now he'd just let it go. At least she'd made it clear it was not a romantic interlude.

She'd nicely set the dining-room table — that she mentioned she hardly ever used and he understood that completely — with china and gleaming silverware. He doubted she used that day to day either and he brought the wine to the table while she brought out the food.

The chicken was delicious, in a sauce laced with brandy and cream, and the potatoes crispy and perfect, even the salad light and yet balanced enough to stand up to the entrée. He was a fan. The conversation did not include anything about the case, the potential stalker, or Anna, for which he was grateful because the latter he would rather not discuss.

An unexplained nervousness became clear after they finished and cleared the plates. Then they sat down again at her suggestion in the living room and Stephanie looked at him and visibly squared her shoulders. "I'm thirty-one."

Mystified as to why that announcement had just been made, he raised his brows. "I know how old you are, Steph."

"I want to have a baby."

Whatever he expected her to say it wasn't that.

The confusion must have showed. "Oh?"

"Okay, that was put so poorly, but cut me some slack, please, because this isn't easy." She did the thing when she swept her hair behind her ear again. That single graceful movement captivated him every single time.

He said, "I'm not following, but occasionally that does happen. You are pointing this out, why?"

"Would you consider it?" She shut her eyes. "Oh hell, that's worse, but I've never done this before. Let me try again. You are intelligent, attractive, healthy, and I would know exactly what I would be getting."

The light dawned and he felt like an idiot but then again, he definitely was blindsided. "So you'd like *my* participation in this process?"

"Yes. No strings attached. No financial responsibility, no parental expectations. I could go to an alternative route, but it seems so impersonal and I know you and . . ."

She trailed off, her usual self-confidence not evident at all, gazing at him with uncertainty and the vulnerability in her expression was out of character.

He wanted to laugh incredulously at the situation but doubted that would be appreciated. "I guess I want to make

75

sure I truly understand by stating it clearly. You want a child and for me to be the one to help make it happen?"

"It's a very personal request. I completely understand if you say no . . ."

He completely understood how difficult it was to walk out on that shaky limb. He was about to do it.

"An unequivocal yes on one condition." He got up and went over and took the wine glass from her hand, set it on the coffee table, and pulled her to her feet. "Can we do it the old-fashioned way?"

And he kissed her.

Passionately, his arm around her waist, pulling her close, not a gentle get-to-know-you kiss, but a lover's embrace, full indication of what he wanted. He was gratified when she responded like he hoped she would, her lips parting, her arms going around his neck, and at the end of it, she looked into his eyes and murmured, "Hmm, I was hoping for the old-fashioned way."

Music to his ears for sure.

His mouth grazed the delicate line of her jaw. "Think of how convincing it will be to whoever is watching that you're involved with someone if I spend the night."

That there were some serious ethical issues with this for both of them was not in question. However he really was worried about Stephanie's safety so it was better he was there, that was true.

And that he really wanted this was not in question.

She felt soft and perfect against him. "You are rationalizing."

"Guilty as charged."

"I'll make coffee in the morning."

"Now, that's an offer I can't refuse. Free coffee? I'm all for that."

"Upstairs then?"

"I'm all in for that too."

She led the way and he followed willingly to say the least. It was what he'd wanted for a long time.

Her bedroom was pale blues with a patterned rug on the floor and she switched on the lamp as the rain tapped at the windows. She reached for the hem of her blouse and pulled it up over her head.

It was interesting to be seduced for a purpose, Trey thought with some measure of insight. It was hardly like he wasn't willing one hundred plus percent, and most young men — he wasn't sure if he qualified for that any longer at thirty-two — went through life trying to not get the wrong girl pregnant, but with Stephanie he was truly on board with it.

Not the wrong girl.

She was supple shadows and highlighted curves. As both of them removed their clothes and he joined her on the four-poster bed, the result was whispers, tentative exploration, and a new knowledge. When it was over he was fairly sure he'd had one of the most satisfying sensual experiences of his lifetime.

Maybe for her too. She ran her fingertips down his bare back and whispered in a muted voice, "I think this might have been one of the best reckless decisions I've ever made."

"No disagreement here."

Her hair spilled over the pillowslip, her gaze searching, the tips of her bare breasts touching his chest. "Why do I think this is going to be more complicated than it was when I sat down and made a short list of men I thought I might ask for this particular favor?"

"There was a list?"

"Of course. I think things through." Then she laughed, which was an interesting — and very nice — sensation since they were still in a very intimate position. "Yours was the only name on it, but it was still a list."

He kissed her softly. "How lucky am I you are so meticulous."

"Not lucky for you in court when I'm meticulous."

That he had to acknowledge. "True enough."

God help him, he was really in love with her and it was a serious conflict of interest.

CHAPTER TEN

Obsession is a difficult thing to control. I've always struggled with it. Another child's toy I wanted, a certain teacher that seemed to think I was worth extra attention, a friend who talked about me behind my back . . .

It could be good or bad.

The definition is to me a compulsion to do irrational acts because you can't stop thinking about something or someone.

There's the phrase, just let it go.

I can't seem to process that.

* * *

Anna was at her desk when the tall man came into her office. She recognized him with a twinge of curiosity as to why he was paying her a visit.

"Detective Bailey."

"Ms. Hernandez." He gestured at a chair. "May I have a word?"

"Of course." She was taken by surprise but it was pretty early in the morning. The coffee maker was still sputtering away — she pointed at it. "It's almost done. Would you like a cup?"

"That would be great. The stuff at the sheriff's office is so bad I can stand it, but only if desperate."

"I make my own, so you are safe. A mountain blend I really like."

He sat down, long legs, cowboy boots — garb like he was starring in a western movie — and she wondered how he got away with it. He didn't look much like a detective but then again he had the air of a competent man with a purpose.

She poured the coffee. "This is about Colin, that's a given."

"Correct. I'm happy to say, that's the only triple homicide case on my radar right now. I've located his father."

She handed him the mug and sank down in her chair, staring at him. After a moment, she asked, "And will he be happy or unhappy with this news?"

Chris Bailey smiled at her and he had quite a nice smile. Actually, he was quite an attractive man with all that tousled blond hair, those intense blue eyes and the casual air. "That is a perfect response. Your first thought is for your charge."

"Of course."

"God bless you for that."

She got it. "Not all social workers are created equal, neither are all detectives . . . so you stopped by to tell me in person?" She picked up a pen. "I assume you have his name and address."

"When I can exchange information with your office, I will."

But not now?

"The arraignment is tomorrow." She said the words in clear protest. "I will need to talk to him."

"I think that's taken care of."

"Trey."

He didn't confirm or deny. "I need permission to talk to Colin freely and alone if you will agree. I believe there's a conversation he and I have to have one-on-one that will never happen if you are in the room."

"What about his lawyer?"

79

"I have permission for that to be waived as well."

"I don't think his father has the ability to give that."

"That's why I'm here."

"Trey agreed to this?" She was surprised, but if she understood her ex-husband better, maybe they'd still be married. When it came to how to conduct himself within the letter of law, he did know what he was doing.

"He did."

She took a drink from her own cup, thinking it over. "Explain to me, Detective, why you expect this will help. Convince me."

He leaned forward, his face earnest. "Look, this is how it is going to go down. Stephanie St. James is going to walk in with charges of multiple homicides, fleeing the scene of a crime with a credible witness to verify, tampering with evidence and obstruction of justice. I'm guessing maybe just going second degree on the murder charges, but either way, Colin goes to prison if a jury agrees with her. All Austin has is he's a nice boy, an athlete and good student who refuses to explain anything. Your ex-husband is a very good defense lawyer, but I don't see how he can win this one. A young man runs out of a house with the proverbial smoking gun and gets rid of it. No visible breaking and entry. I believe the average person would think he's guilty."

He sat back and drank some coffee.

The hell of it was she agreed. She'd lain in bed last night telling herself even Trey couldn't do it. As convinced she was that in the courtroom any defense he presented could win the case, maybe not this one.

Anna thought she was a reasonable person, so she took in a breath. "Explain to me why you think you can make Colin talk to you when he won't to anyone else, and the answer is a yes. I do care about what happens next."

"I have a theory about what is going on and maybe he'll talk and maybe he won't, but let me give it a try?"

She looked at Chris Bailey and agreed. "I'm going to trust you have good instincts and if it might help that child, that's fine with me. My major was in psychology, and I learned we are not fully functioning adults mentally until we are twenty-five and that is still quite a few years away for Colin. He's a child. Keep it in mind. Don't intimidate him. Give me your word."

He looked back steadily. "What you can trust is that I'm trying to solve this case because I don't think he is guilty of the crimes he is going to be charged with, so we are on the same team. If he did do it, I'd be surprised. I don't like being wrong."

"In other words, you aren't looking to wring a confession out of him."

"Not a confession of murder."

"Then what?"

"Let's see what he has to say."

What the hell did that mean? Anna asked in cynical amusement, "Detective Bailey, are you always so cryptic?"

His mouth curved. "Uh, I've been accused of a lot of things, some of which I am guilty, but I don't know if cryptic has ever been slung my way before."

"I'll make a phone call giving you permission to visit Colin for an interview since I'm getting the impression his father is not anxious to take over as custodian."

"He has kept it on the down-low so far, don't you agree?"

"There's no doubt about that," she muttered in agreement. "He's been out of his child's life from conception as far as I know, since Colin doesn't even know him."

"He has a reason. I don't know if it is a good one, but a reason. He has stepped up enough that I do believe he cares."

She lifted a brow. "Someday tell me?"

"That's a date. I'll buy you a drink, I think I owe you." He finished his coffee and stood. "If you'll make that call, I'd appreciate it. Let me know when I can talk to him?"

"I will."

He stopped just short of the doorway and turned. "One thing I can say for Austin is in my opinion he has good taste in women."

Nonplussed, she watched him leave and had the feeling he'd just paid her — and Stephanie — a compliment.

Apparently he hadn't missed that dynamic.

He was, after all, a detective.

And a pretty damned attractive one.

Not a bad start to her work day.

* * *

Work a hypothesis was something he shouldn't do.

An idea postulated on a few facts that might be plausible evidence of a truth.

That was called in more generic terms speculation.

Not allowed in law enforcement, but it happened. He'd solved a few cases by breaking that rule.

In this instance, he was decently sure he was on the right track.

Colin looked happy to see him, or maybe it was just a treat to not be confined with his brethren who were also accused of crimes, though he probably was kept apart given the severity of the charges likely to be filed against him.

Good. If the kid needed someone to talk to Chris was the perfect choice.

He took the opposite seat at the sterile table in a sterile room. "Detective."

"Colin, how are you doing?"

"Okay."

"Both Ms. Hernandez and Trey Austin agreed to let me talk to you one-on-one, just to be sure you know that."

"Yeah, they both called me."

Chris didn't fold his hands together because that was something he'd learned early meant a sense of power, and it happened in about every movie he'd ever seen and he wanted this to be just two people having a chat. Instead, he sat in his chair and leaned back. "Someone called *me*."

"Oh?" He looked suddenly wary but also hopeful.

"They didn't identify themselves but said they might have information to help on your case." Chris considered him. "Your generation is tech savvy, but I don't know if you all realize how sophisticated our system is if you call a line connected to a phone provided by the sheriff's office or any other public law enforcement venue."

"Venue? What's that mean?"

There was no doubt Chris gave a disbelieving laugh. "Nice try, Colin. You know exactly what it means because you're a smart kid, and even if you didn't you'd figure it out from context. I know whose phone was used, but I don't think that person is the one who actually called — probably a friend of hers. According to her parents, Betsy is a popular girl with a wide social circle. They couldn't narrow it down for me but I know where she goes to school."

"I don't know anyone named Betsy."

"But someone you know does. You have a girlfriend you've been seeing on the quiet, don't you? What's the problem? Her parents don't like you?"

"That's one hell of an understatement."

That was progress anyway.

"Tell me."

He just looked away. "I want to, but I managed to get most of my family killed. I'm not going to risk her."

Maybe when he was seventeen he was that idealistic. Romeo and Juliet were younger than the stubborn young man sitting in front of him when they committed suicide in the name of love, but that was fiction.

At least he was talking.

Chris tried for the voice of reason. "Stephanie St. James doesn't want to do it, but she's going to hit you with serious charges because you're it. I couldn't agree more. You look guilty because of quite a few factors."

"I know."

"Trey Austin is good, but you know what. I'm good too. I'm much more likely to get you off the hook. Just tell me what is at stake here."

"Two more lives."

Oh shit.

He didn't need to be a detective for that one. Chris ran his hand through his hair and assessed this new angle. "Your girlfriend is pregnant?"

"I know. I don't need the lecture." He looked away, but then met his eyes, not defiant but defensive. "It just happened."

"I'll leave that to someone else. I'm not into lectures. Was she the one that called?"

"I would guess, but I'm serious here. She's in danger if I don't go to jail."

He'd discount it but this was the first real information Colin had offered that he knew of in this entire investigation.

"From who?"

"A person who is seriously messed up."

"Be specific?"

"You heard what I said earlier, right?"

"I heard it. I'm just wondering why you won't just give me a name. I'm a police officer and you know what? I've arrested murderers before."

"I don't have any proof. I just *know*."

"You don't have any proof because you got rid of the gun."

Colin shook his head and didn't give an inch. "I've never said that I did."

A definitive moment. How to handle this was crucial because that was why he wanted this opportunity to not have a gathering but instead a conversation. Chris just kept his tone moderate. "No you haven't. It makes me hopeful you know where it is because if you tell me and I can tie it back to the individual that murdered — that's a powerful word — your mother, grandmother, and stepfather — I will be able to protect this girl you are willing to sacrifice your future for."

"How?"

"Weapons can be traced usually unless you are really good at meticulously planning ahead. My impression was this was a crime of passion to the extent the person was entirely ticked off and did it impulsively, because for some reason they didn't take the gun with them. Give it to me and I will take them out of the equation."

Colin sat there, but Chris was pretty good at waiting out a witness and there was progress.

"If I do . . . I mean . . . I just picked it up. I didn't know what had happened. My fingerprints are on it."

"Yeah, and maybe someone else's are too."

"I know this person has done some fairly other serious things before . . . I mean bad. Crazy stuff."

Whoa. That was information he didn't expect. "Like?"

"Other murders maybe."

That made him take a moment. He finally said, "And how do you know this?"

"My girlfriend told me."

"Can I have a name?"

Colin shook his head.

The problem was, he understood. The kid was understandably scared. He'd walked in on a serious scene of three dead bodies, all people who were important in his young life. Chris had seen it firsthand. It wasn't a happy memory for him either and it hadn't been personal.

He rubbed his jaw and thought about it. "Okay, let's do it this way. Give me the gun and I'll figure it out on my own. I won't question anyone without talking to you first again and am ready to make an arrest. Is that a deal?"

Colin looked at him and said, "Only if you promise me I'll be charged with murder at the arraignment today."

CHAPTER ELEVEN

My dreams are dark and they always have been.

Confusing images I can't interpret when I wake, a serious delineation between what might be real and what is just fantastical.

Surely most of it isn't true.

Or I hope not.

* * *

It had been interesting waking up to Trey's much taller body taking up most of her bed as both the alarms on their phones went off at six o'clock. She went downstairs to make the promised coffee and Stephanie took this opportunity to wake up and assess her interesting decision to sleep with her best friend's ex-husband.

At some point, she would have to deal with Anna's feelings about it, and that was a serious consideration.

The tentative olive branch of dinner together after a distant year of separation was going to vanish in an instant.

Stephanie was very cognizant this had been her decision and she would probably pay for it in the friendship department, but then again she was an adult and unattached, and so was Trey.

Still, complicated.

Life was in general.

He came down, tousled and in last night's clothes, but he hadn't anticipated spending the night either. "You delivered on your promise. Thank goodness. I have a full day."

She handed him a mug from a cabinet above the coffee pot. "Help yourself and I think we both do. I have to meet with Hanover before the arraignment."

"It's a formality but part of the process."

"You do know who you're talking to, right?"

"Intimately."

They just looked at each other.

He spoke first, losing that attractive smile. "Professionally, nothing for me has changed and I assume you feel the same way. We've known each other for quite a while and faced each other in court without any problem. Yes, we are both lawyers but we don't have the same job and we are entitled to a personal life outside our profession."

It was a reasonable argument, but they had crossed an interesting line the night before, and she had to admit she was looking forward to crossing it again. There had always been chemistry, and on a physical level it had been combustible.

Professionally she agreed with him. They could handle that.

Emotionally she wasn't positive where it was going.

He left after he finished his coffee and she took a shower and got ready for work, thinking about it.

Anna had known it. Nothing had ever been said to her directly, but she'd known.

Damn, she thought as she drove to the office.

What she didn't expect was to walk into a meeting and find Detective Bailey there in Ed Hanover's office. Her boss was a very conservative man, reserved and well-respected, but a good attorney in many respects in that he liked to always win. Getting him to ever take a chance on the conviction in question was a long shot.

And she had a compelling argument for murder two.

But she wasn't going to make it.

Hanover, business-like as usual, gestured at a chair. "Have a seat, Stephanie. You know Detective Bailey."

"I . . . do." She sat down and waited for someone to say something because she certainly didn't know what was going on.

Distinguished and always in charge, Hanover nodded and glanced at the clock on the wall. "You're due in court in less than two hours. How are you going to charge?"

She glanced at Bailey again, and then just said it out loud. "I'm a little puzzled here. Since when does a county detective sit in on a meeting in the prosecutor's office like this? No offense intended, Detective, I just have a feeling I've walked into something that I might need to know about."

"I have the murder weapon." Bailey was as polite as always.

"Oh?" She had to admit that made her take a second to reconsider. It was significant. "Evidence that incriminates or exonerates?"

"Neither one."

There was no help for it, Stephanie lifted her hands. "So we are in the same place?"

Bailey said mildly, "Not quite. Colin's prints are on it, but we expected it. He's never denied that."

"Care to explain?"

"I need time."

So the answer was no.

She talked to Hanover directly then, stating her case. "I know this is opposite of how you run this office because I'm sure I can get a conviction, but I'd like to just charge this particular accused with tampering with evidence and obstruction of justice and let that stand. I don't think he murdered anyone and it is still under investigation. I believe murder in the second degree would fly with a jury, but it would be a miscarriage of justice."

"No. Charge him with murder." That was Bailey, his voice cool and assured. "Please. It is at his request."

"*What?*" She couldn't help it, she stared at him, wondering if she'd heard correctly.

Hanover lifted his shoulders. "I think you now know why Detective Bailey is sitting in on this meeting."

It took a moment to collect her poise but Stephanie said with what she thought admirable calm, "Let me get this straight. The accused, Colin Simon, *wants* me to bring formal charges of second-degree murder against him and both of you agree I should? Because even with his high-profile lawyer defending, I'll win and he'll spend a lot of time in prison."

Bailey looked unfazed. "I know it seems like we are walking this backward, but Colin gave me the weapon and some other interesting information, not to mention, he isn't protecting the murderer, he's protecting the next potential victims. So let's publicly charge him, make it look like we've solved the case, and I will do my very best to arrest the right person, and then charges can be dropped."

It was Hanover that said, "I'm for this position."

Surprise was an understatement.

She had to give Bailey credit, Hanover was not easy to convince to stray from a straightforward traditional approach. She looked at her boss. "You support this?"

"Yes, I do."

"Okay, gentlemen, I'll do it." She stood, but then couldn't help it and turned to Bailey. "I walked in here afraid I was going to get pushback because I didn't want to file charges. You're sure?"

"What specific question are you asking me? No, don't bother to answer that, because I am going to tell you. I'll do my best to solve this case so we never see a courtroom. That I can promise. I'm not going to let an innocent kid go to prison for murder if I can help it."

She really looked at him. "Detective Bailey, even Trey Austin might not be able to tear my prosecution apart."

"My word on it I'll do my best to give him ammunition to make a motion to dismiss."

"You know something else." She said it as a statement not a question, because the vibe was definitely there.

"Yes, but you need to file charges." Bailey's smile was rueful. "I feel ridiculous saying this, but I pretty much promised him you'd do it. Please don't make me break my word. It was the only way he'd give me the evidence we need."

"Well, shit, you're not going to tell me."

Hanover actually looked amused she swore out loud because that was hardly her. "Stephanie, just so you know, I'll be second counsel on this. Your case, but obviously not a usual one."

You'd think that would be a relief but it wasn't necessarily. What it meant was instead of sitting down with another attorney to discuss how they'd handle the case and exchanging opinions, she'd be sitting down with her boss to get instruction on how he wanted her to handle it.

He didn't do that often.

There was definitely something important no one was telling her.

Why?

The frustrating thing was she'd bet Trey knew and wouldn't tell her either.

She gave them her best polite smile. "Excuse me. I don't want to be late for court."

* * *

The man who sat across from him was a very much older version of his son, but for someone who knew them both, the resemblance was unmistakable.

It made Trey wonder if he and Stephanie did have a child together, would he — or she — have fair hair, or his dark coloring . . . it wasn't something that had particularly occurred to him, but then again, he hadn't anticipated her request either.

No complaints, but still, new to him and he'd agreed only because of how he felt about her, not with thinking it through, the emotional and physical elements eclipsing the intellectual consideration.

Senator Grayson regarded him and said, "I wanted to meet with you first. What is happening?"

"I'm sure you'll agree Bailey is good at his job."

"That was not a call I wanted."

Trey was fairly politic in his speech because he had to be, but then again he was also realistic. "Don't worry. He's not a loose cannon as a detective. He's just focused. I was there when he asked Colin if he was protecting his biological father. Colin replied he didn't even know you, but that Bailey didn't leave that stone unturned does not surprise me. Neither does the fact he uncovered the truth. If it is any consolation, I believe he's taken you off the table as a possible suspect. He just wants to know if you might help him help your son."

"I was a suspect?" The man looked stunned.

"Of course."

He exhaled. "Oh, Jesus. I would never have imagined that."

"Bailey is good and he's not interested in the spotlight. He's interested in justice and protecting future possible victims."

"If you're telling me the truth, I agree."

"So, at the arraignment this afternoon Colin was charged with three counts of second-degree murder."

"But he didn't do it?" There was true concern in his eyes.

"I most certainly don't think he did. Colin is a decent kid. More than that, he's someone trying to figure all this out adrift and alone at his age. He's hiding something, and he isn't telling anyone what it is, but I don't think it is guilt in the murders of those three people."

"You know him better than I do. That kills me." Grayson looked away, his expression tight. "He's my only child. That he even exists would devastate my wife, so please understand I'm willing to take responsibility, but it isn't simple."

91

"It will never come from our firm or I doubt the sheriff's office either. You represent these people. You know what it is like here. We keep things close here in Tennessee."

His smile held a hint of ironic acknowledgment when he looked back. "I do know that about this fine state."

He wasn't a law enforcement officer, but this man was his client to the extent he had reached out to ask him to represent Colin and was paying the attorney fees, so Trey did say with some directness, "I think you should be prepared to be asked if there is any chance your wife does know about your son."

It took a moment for the implication of that question to hit him. "No, no. Loraine would never seek vengeance by harming anyone. If she knew, she would blame me, and in truth, she has a reason to, though I'm not proud to admit I was unfaithful. She would be hurt and I own it."

"Could those murders have been politically motivated?"

He did think about it for a moment, tense in his chair in Trey's office. "There are some crazy people out there and of course I have received my fair share of hate mail as a public figure, but I'm pretty moderate. The truth is other than the bank officer that handles his child support and his trust fund, no one really knows Colin is related to me in any way."

"Unless Roxanne Gaines had told someone."

"I'm actually going to doubt she did." Grayson said it with some measure of conviction. "She was a reasonable, intelligent person and had the same attitude about the affair. It was a lapse in judgment for both of us. She had no desire to destroy my marriage. We had an amicable agreement that I would provide support and she would raise our child. I trusted she would be a good mother and it seems to me she really fulfilled that part of our devil's bargain, and she trusted I would keep my word as well."

It was really interesting to be having this conversation on a personal level, since Trey had essentially agreed to a similar arrangement, except Stephanie had made it clear she expected nothing but his participation in conception.

That he wanted much more than that was a discussion he and Stephanie needed to have, but it was still so new he was not willing to push it yet.

It was certainly not Trey's place to counsel the man, but he did say, "He has a caring social worker that is on his side one hundred percent, but Colin is pretty alone. That Detective Bailey is still pursuing this means he's not convinced of his guilt. Even the district attorney who brought the charges isn't convinced, but Colin is being stubborn. Maybe a voice of reason might work."

"He doesn't know me."

"He's been looking in the mirror for seventeen years. When you walked into my office, I knew you were his father. He looks a lot like you. He's been waiting — and I suspect wanting — to meet you for a long time. He might listen."

The senator smiled thinly. "Alright, you are probably worth the money I'm paying you because you make a good argument and I guess I'll talk to him. I want to post his bail."

"It was set at one million. That's only because the prosecuting attorney argued to get it lower since she really didn't want to charge him in the first place. The judge suggested twice that amount."

Colin's father didn't blink, but then again, he knew it would be high. He rose and nodded. When he got to the door, he turned. "Why *did* Ms. St. James charge him?"

So he had been paying close attention if he knew Stephanie was in charge of the case.

"Because your son wanted her to file formal charges or else he wouldn't hand over the murder weapon." Trey said firmly, "Do you see why you need to talk to him? Maybe he'll tell you why."

"I don't know. I've been a father for seventeen years. I've just never been a parent."

There was a poignant moment of self-contemplation when the senator left.

Trey saw on his phone Stephanie had finally responded to his dinner invitation.

Sorry, busy day. What did you have in mind?

He could do steaks and baked potatoes and a pre-made salad was easy enough. He wasn't a good cook, but not totally without culinary skills.

My house? Same time?

Okay, sounds good. My turn to bring the wine.

That was something anyway. No regrets after the night before yet.

He suspected she had had a difficult afternoon. Bringing charges when he was aware she didn't really want to do it had to be a confrontation of ethics and sensibility and if Stephanie was nothing else, she was a compassionate, decent person.

I'll make sure there are a couple of glasses waiting.

CHAPTER TWELVE

I was twelve when I realized I was a little different. No, maybe ten, it is a blur to me. The years blend together in an interesting way.

I did something bad.

Really bad, I think.

I don't remember it all that well.

It might be I'd rather not recall the event.

* * *

He agreed probably Carter should do most of the interview.

Hands down.

His partner was more experienced and if it came down to it, just plain more diplomatic.

He and a U.S. senator would do better than Chris with his casual approach.

"Son," Sheriff Lawrence said with his usual dry humor, "you operate on the edge, which works most of the time, but not always. Not everyone can solve a problem just because they have their facts in hand and will not back down — even if it means walking Main Street with their pistol holstered but ready for the quick draw."

"I'm supposed to have my weapon ready to be drawn at all times, sir."

"Don't be cheeky with me, Bailey."

Chris liked Lawrence, who was definitely old-school. "Right. I'll let Carter do the talking."

"It isn't every day this office sees a visit from a member of the United States Senate."

"It isn't every day we *need* to talk to someone from Washington."

"I see you didn't dress up for the visit."

It was true. He wore his usual jeans, boots and a denim shirt. "The man is from Tennessee. I'm sure he'll forgive the lack of formality."

The sheriff shook his head. "This is your case and you seem to be managing it, so I'll leave you to it and not ask questions."

"No mention of it to the media."

"I completely agree with that. You know full well I hate that crap anyway. This county office is not a high-school hallway. I'll make sure Doreen understands that."

Doreen handled the desk and calls that weren't dispatch and was invaluable, and she certainly would note Senator Grayson's visit — she might mention it to her many friends.

Chris had definitely confirmed low key, no press, if he could just ask a few questions. Colin's father had certainly agreed that a discreet venue in his home state would be better than having two detectives visit his office in Washington, D.C., which probably was, as the sheriff so eloquently put it, like a gossipy high-school hallway, so he'd made the trip.

Considering his son had been charged on three separate counts of murder, Chris's opinion was it was the least he could do. At least Stephanie St. James had dropped the tampering with evidence and obstruction of justice charges since he'd turned over the gun, but those were paltry compared to the ones she'd brought forth.

"We aren't actually meeting here, so don't mention it to Doreen."

It was true, an hour later he pulled into the wooded driveway of his river cabin that was pretty isolated, which to

Chris was a great deal of its appeal. No luxury, but lots of quiet and nature.

Not one single soul would see the senator meet with two police detectives, and there was a familiar car parked near the steps down to the single door.

Carter had already taken the senator inside — the place was unlocked, Chris just thought it was pointless as there was no way to prevent someone from breaking in, and there was nothing of value to steal anyway. They were seated at the square table and someone had apparently brought a bottle of Tennessee's finest and found a tumbler on one of the shelves. The senator had poured himself a glass.

Grayson stood to shake hands and pointed at the bottle. "I figured since this was an informal meeting this particular evening called for some fortification. Thanks for this setting. Nice place. Help yourself if you like and then you can ask your questions. Since Detective Carter is driving, I figured I might as well imbibe."

Chris wasn't at all sure the place qualified as nice, and informal was a very apt description considering the rustic setting, but it was private and why he suggested it, and no doubt why Grayson agreed to an unusual location.

Carter was jacket and tie, his thinning hair perfectly brushed, and the two men were close to the same age. Both of them outdistanced Chris by about two decades and Lawrence was probably right about letting Carter take charge of this even if he'd been the one putting in the legwork and set everything up. His partner was a really good cop, that wasn't in question, and he looked the part a lot more than Chris ever would, if he was honest with himself.

He wasn't amiss to having a companionable drink, especially with the cool crisp air and the river moving slowly in the background. It was after five o'clock. "I'll have a drink, thanks. I'm staying the night here."

Of course Carter wasn't drinking, because he was so by the book it wasn't funny, but if he had to call it Chris bet he would like one.

The senator watched him get out a glass and his expression held some cynical amusement. "So you are Detective Bailey."

"Yeah, I know my call to your office was kind of off the cuff, but I really wanted to get your attention." He splashed some very expensive whiskey into his glass and did his best to seem apologetic.

He wasn't.

"Detective, you left a message that said, 'Eighteen years ago you made a decision and someone who isn't quite that age yet might pay a price that will end their life. Don't think it is possible to ignore it because I am persistent. Call me. I need to talk to you'."

"I was trying to make it impossible for anyone but you to understand what I meant." He said it mildly, and he took a sip of some really good bourbon.

"As an ultimatum it was effective." Grayson added quietly, "I appreciate the discretion of your office."

"You didn't commit a crime other than a transgression that might bother your moral conscience and mistakes like that are made all the time. I'm only concerned with those folks that do really bad things. Triple homicide qualifies."

"Folks? Maybe I've spent too much time in Washington." The senator looked amused but it was fleeting as the subject was hardly humorous. "I do miss living here."

Well, he was from this area and people referred to each other like that.

Carter sat down at the table and the look on his face said, *I could swear Lawrence told me, and you, I was supposed to be lead on this.*

True.

The senator went on. "If I can help I will, of course. The first thing I did was go see Colin's lawyer and he told me about the charges presented to the court."

"Did he tell you that the only way your son would turn over the murder weapon he concealed was if he was charged with murder?" Carter asked it in measured tones.

"Yes. Why would he do that?"

"We'd really like for you to present that question to him."

"Trey Austin said you asked if my son was protecting me. His answer was he doesn't know me. Why do you think he would explain anything to me?" There was regret in Grayson's voice. "I don't even know if Roxanne ever told him I contributed financially as he was growing up, or if he knows I was the one who retained a good attorney for him. I care, I just don't want to lose my marriage and live through the press nightmare because I am such a public figure. Please admit if the illegitimate child of a member of the U.S. Senate is on trial for the murder of three people, it will draw a lot of attention even if just for the sensational aspect of it. He's pretty young to be examined under that ruthless microscope."

Chris thought he certainly had a point and he had no idea if Colin would resent his father's absence in his life, not care one way or the other, or be happy to finally have an answer to what must be a lingering question always in his mind. He had been there when Colin said he accepted his mother's very generic explanation and there had been at least a hint of frustration in the young man's voice.

Who could blame him? There was a reason even adopted kids raised by two loving people wanted to find out about their real parents.

"Is it possible your wife does actually know you have a child with someone else?" Carter was direct and he did that well. "Surely she has access to your financial information and you just said you provided for him since his birth. I'd wonder if my wife was making regular payments of some sort to a person in Tennessee."

Outside the wind rustled the leaves, otherwise it was dead quiet. The senator shook his head. "I had an accountant handle it discreetly and I have been married to her for a long time. If she found out, she'd have confronted me. She wanted children, it just didn't happen. Multiple miscarriages and she was devastated each time."

It actually provided a motive if she had somehow discovered the truth, so that was interesting information.

Carter never operated on motive however. "How often did you talk to Roxanne Gaines?"

"Directly? Never after she came to my office to tell me personally she was pregnant, but we had ended the affair well before that already and after that I just used my accountant. It was amicable, she was a very nice person and there was no avarice. I offered financial support because she was unmarried at the time, and of course, it was an unplanned pregnancy. The least I could do. That was almost two decades ago." His smile was thin. "I'm not proud of it, but truthfully, my wife and I were going through a rocky patch. It doesn't excuse me, but it is why it happened. Of course, I continued to provide for our child even after Roxanne married Joe Gaines because Colin was my responsibility, not his. He was divorced and supporting a daughter already."

Unfortunately, Chris could see it in another light. "Is there anyone you can think of that might want to get to you through your son?"

"To my knowledge no one knows I have one except the two of you."

"*I* figured it out."

Grayson considered him. "You are, by all accounts, a pretty decent detective."

"I try. Can you consider my question carefully? I think this is personal."

* * *

Anna followed the directions carefully and found the place easily enough since it had the only lights in the dark in the woods.

She parked and knew she was running late, the wind was really picking up and why she wasn't simply doing this at her office or even at the sheriff's office became apparent the minute Detective Bailey came out to greet her. "Thanks for coming all this way."

"Is there some reason for this subterfuge?"

"Yeah, there actually is. He's inside."

There was no question that she gave him a questioning look, but then she understood when she walked into the simple cabin and saw the man sitting at the table.

Had to be Colin Simon's father, the resemblance was so marked. Never had she made the connection before, but then the man stood and offered his hand. "Senator Grayson. Ms. Hernandez, I want to thank you for helping Colin."

The pieces came together at least a little bit.

Okay, Colin's biological father was a high-profile senior senator in the United States Senate.

No wonder this was not necessarily clandestine, but at least a remote meeting.

She wasn't precisely shocked, but off balance, for sure. She managed to murmur, "Well, of course. He's a young man in a very bad situation. He definitely needs an advocate."

Bailey motioned to a chair. "Have a seat. Can I get you something to drink? Let's see, water, beer or coffee, but my coffee isn't as good yours. That's about it here in the sticks."

"Or some very good bourbon." The senator pointed at the bottle with a charming smile. "I take it you made the drive straight from work and I appreciate it."

She was still dressed in slacks and silk blouse, not to mention shoes with a heel, which she despised but did look professional. At the moment she was glad she looked the part, but longed for worn jeans and her favorite flannel shirt, especially considering the surroundings. "I'll take a glass of bourbon, thank you. I had quite the afternoon."

Some fortitude might be needed for this conversation in an isolated cabin on a windy October night with two detectives and a prominent politician. She was out of her element. Social work included a lot of things, but not usually this sort of meeting.

Bailey got out a glass, muttered something, rinsed it and wiped it out, and said with a hint of humor, "I don't dust often enough. I just come here to fish and relax."

So this must be the cabin Stephanie had mentioned. It definitely had a masculine air to it considering no curtains, and the décor screamed Tennessee backwoods.

The senator poured her a drink and handed it over. "My son is going to make bail. I'm not letting him sit in jail."

The point of this meeting suddenly became clear. She took a sip and though she really wasn't much of a judge of bourbon, it was very smooth. "I have to find a place for him to go, and as you can imagine, most foster parents aren't interested in a young man accused of murder."

"So what are you going to do?"

As he'd be a natural choice to step in, she just looked at him in consternation and then regrouped.

"If he was eighteen, he'd just be released and it would fall on him to find a place to live. But he isn't."

"Senator, don't give him money, because that might be your first impulse, but he's got to be one scared kid." That was Detective Carter, the only one apparently not imbibing in an alcoholic beverage, always direct and reasonable. "He might decide to run."

It was Bailey that said, "He can stay with me if that would work. I have an extra bedroom and I assume as a law enforcement officer, I would qualify as a reasonable choice. He knows me."

Anna was surprised, but then again, maybe she wasn't. He seemed like just the sort of person who might offer up something like that, and clearly he didn't think Colin was guilty. He probably also slept lightly and at a guess, not that much, so he wouldn't be afraid of a teenaged boy taking him off guard.

Anna liked the unusual suggestion. "It would make my job easier. I feel confident everyone would agree to that idea despite your age."

His brows went up. "My age?"

"You are a little bit young, Detective, to be in charge of a seventeen-year-old boy since you aren't old enough to be his parent. What are you, twenty-eight maybe?"

"Try again and don't let my boyish good looks fool you. Thirty-one. *He's* old enough to be a parent."

There was no doubt she didn't like the information just imparted, but the slight flirtation was noted.

"What?" The senator looked like someone had hit him with a coal scuttle. "I hope you don't mean what I think you mean."

"Yeah, he wouldn't give me her name." Bailey simply looked introspective. "That's who he's protecting and the threat seems to be significant enough he's willing to go to prison. So what we need is to be able to figure this out quickly and if I'm the one he has to rely on he and I will have a lot of time to talk. There were other prints on that weapon and he's the key. I ran them through the database and they don't register. This person has been operating under the radar."

"Filed-off registration number on the weapon and the ballistics match our victims." Detective Carter nodded, looking like he agreed. "I'm with you since you persuaded him to hand over the gun. I think it is solid logic he might finally tell you who she is if just to protect her. In that light since you are younger, it might make him more likely to talk to you."

There was no question Anna felt like a second character in a crime show series. "This girl is in danger?"

"Yes." Bailey said it with all due practicality. "And anyone else this person might hurt, true? If you walked into a house and killed three people in cold blood, you're dangerous, period. To everyone. I want them off the street."

He had a valid point.

"Why does Colin think this?" Anna couldn't help it. "Did he say?"

"He said he managed to get his entire family killed and two more lives were at stake."

Senator Grayson muttered, "Oh God, he said that? He's seventeen. That's too young to carry that kind of guilt. Maybe he'll talk to me, or maybe he won't, but I'll try tomorrow when he's released on bond."

Better late than never, Anna thought grimly, but she was all too used to dealing with neglected children, not that Colin really fell into that category, because it sounded to her — and from his account as well — he had a happy, well-adjusted upbringing with a caring mother and a stepfather he liked and respected.

That settled, Carter and the senator departed and she sat there trying to decide if she should finish her drink or not because she did have to drive home.

Bailey eyed her with some amusement, apparently able to read minds. "Stay as long as you like. Ms. St. James stayed the night."

"And slept with just your dog according to her." Anna said it with a lifted brow.

"That's correct. I can be a gentleman if I need to be."

It had been a while since she'd been attracted to anyone but Trey, and that was a useless emotion. She'd divorced him for a very good reason and he hadn't argued the decision either. That told her everything she needed to know.

Her impression was that Detective Bailey might be interested in more than just talking about his case.

And that might be reciprocated.

She said, "I'll finish my drink then and stay for a little while."

"I'd like that," he said and smiled. "I didn't bring my dog so I could use the company."

CHAPTER THIRTEEN

Control is important.
It is everything in my opinion.
I just don't have enough of it. I never have.

* * *

Trey met Stephanie at the door with a very memorable kiss
that startled her into almost dropping the two very breakable
bottles of wine.

He took the bag with a compelling smile when he
released her, his arm loosening from around her waist. "That
might have been a little over the top, but I'm glad you're
here."

She responded after she took in a breath, "No apology necessary, I'm happy to be here. My afternoon wasn't
perfect."

"Mine either, so let's not talk about it."

The difference between them was he couldn't talk about
it, at least not with her. No disclosure, it was an echo in her
head.

She looked at him, which was never a hardship, especially when he was casual in faded jeans that emphasized his

lean build and a pullover with the logo of the University of Tennessee that emphasized he had a very nice, muscular body.

"You've lost your mind if you think we aren't going to talk about it. I was forced to file charges this afternoon I wasn't going to file all because your client insisted I do so or he'd continue to hold that murder weapon hostage."

His response was succinct. "I believe you know as much as I do then, if not more. The wine glasses are this way." He pointed. "Shall we?"

Needless to say, he had a very nice house. Expensive neighborhood, large yard, impressive size, high ceilings and a gourmet kitchen from what she could see. Through glass doors there was an in-ground pool visible past a sunroom.

She was sure he could afford it, but why he'd do it was a mystery to her.

"Quite the bachelor pad." It was a dry observation.

"Not my intention when I bought it. I was looking to the future when I decided on this place."

That did silence her, she had to admit.

So he wanted a family? At least it sounded like it.

"Red wine? I'm just grilling steaks."

"Just pour something into my glass, please."

"Have a seat at the bar." He flashed her that signature smile. "I'm serving."

There were bar stools at the fancy island and she took one, brushing back her hair. "I just don't know how to deal with this situation. I can go after any guilty bastard without regret but I have to let you, Bailey, and Carter handle this, and hopefully you will. I feel helpless and I hate it."

He splashed crimson liquid into a wine glass and slid it over to her. "Welcome to the club. Bailey was able to pry out of Colin the murder weapon. I am supposed to be his rock in a rough sea when he's capsized, but he talked to the investigating officer more than me."

She contemplated that statement. "No, he trusts you, I can see it, but Bailey asks the right probing questions. He should be a prosecutor."

"No." He poured a glass for himself and shook his head, a distracting dark errant curl falling attractively over his forehead. "That man wants to pursue criminals, not prosecute or defend them. He's not out for Colin particularly, he has an eye on the guilty party and my client is the ace up his sleeve. We are all programmed for different things."

True enough.

She considered her glass and looked up. "Trey, I can't do this. Bailey better come through. I can't convince a jury to convict that kid. I mean I think I can convince them, I just don't want to."

"As the defending attorney, I support that and will do my best to make sure it doesn't happen."

Her smile was genuine. "Okay, we've discussed it. No more of that. What else do you want to talk about? Opera? I'm really a fan of Italian composers like Verdi, but the Germans aren't so bad—"

"Not opera." He was decisive and amused. "Not my thing since I know zero about it. How about how the Titans are going to do this season? I'm never sure, but hopeful."

"I don't follow football so that doesn't fly either."

"So, let's have a nice dinner — hopefully, though I'm not a stellar cook — and forget it. Have you seen that woman again?"

"The one following me? Not today, but then again I was pretty distracted."

"And if you stay here tonight, that might solve the problem."

She had to laugh, though she had to admit she'd been relieved to not see her. "Are you trying to seduce me?"

"Seduce? Have you been reading romance novels again, Ms. St. James?" He did keep a straight face but his mouth twitched.

"Since about the sixth grade."

"Okay, I guess that's about the age when I found my father's vintage *Playboy* magazines and thumbed through them, so we're even."

"Thumbed through them?"

"Maybe I lingered on a page or two."

"Read the articles?"

"Of course." He did his best to look innocent and failed.

"Glad that is settled." She was laughing and did feel better.

"I try to be honest if nothing else. I'm going to go light the grill if you want to bring your wine out on the deck but it is pretty windy."

The forecast had indicated rain moving in. She declined. "I might just sit here and decompress."

"Do that. I'll be back."

If you stay here tonight . . .

She'd started this, she mused. The wine was nice, which was a good thing as she'd just dashed into the liquor store and grabbed a couple of bottles with labels that caught her eye, which is not how a person should select an expensive beverage.

It wasn't going to be simple, but then again, what relationship ever was.

Daniel had texted her again this afternoon.

It annoyed her, but maybe the woman *was* tied to him. He'd just suggested maybe they could talk sometime, which she had no intention of agreeing to at all. There was nothing to discuss.

She'd ignored it.

Nice music in the background. Chopin. Good wine, a very attractive man fixing her dinner, she was starting to relax.

Until her phone rang. She saw the identity of the caller and answered at once.

"Mrs. Burke?"

"Honey, you weren't home long but that woman put something on your car when you went inside. I was headed out for my walk and the more I thought about it, the more I decided that was what she was doing so I decided just to call you. She was gone when I got back, but so were you."

108

"I . . . see. Well, I'll take a look and thank you so much for letting me know."

"I don't like her hanging around here."

"Me either."

When Trey came back in the door — and he did look tousled from the wind — she asked matter-of-factly, "Why would anyone put a tracking device on my car?"

* * *

He found it fairly easily, though it was hardly his area of expertise, but then had an inner debate about removing the device. Right-hand side, under the back bumper.

It had started to spit rain sideways and they hadn't had dinner yet and the unfriendly skies were lowering.

The steaks were done and resting, the potatoes were still in the oven, and Stephanie had offered to toss the salad together if he'd go take a look. For the moment he left it and went back in the house, running his fingers through his now damp hair.

"Your neighbor is a very observant lady. I'm hardly a mechanic but there's something I don't recognize as being the usual part of a vehicle attached to your undercarriage just below the bumper." He picked up his glass of wine. "I left it. Let's eat dinner and talk about what to do about it."

"Get rid of it." Her lovely eyes were full of outrage.

"Hold on a second and let's think about it. Let me get the potatoes."

He'd not really used the dining room since he'd bought the house and he had to admit it was on the ostentatious side, but the couple who'd built the place had split and just included the table and chairs in the purchase price because they couldn't agree on who would get it, and so yes, he had a table for eight. It wasn't intimate by any stretch so he had set it so they sat next to each other at one end. Neither did he usually get out placemats and the nice dishes he'd been given by his grandmother either, but on this occasion, yes. Usually he just sat at the kitchen counter and ate there, or sometimes at his desk in his home office.

Stephanie followed him with the salad, glanced around and asked, "Just how big of a family are you planning on having?"

His response was smooth. "You tell me."

She was the one who suggested they embark on this journey, so she could hardly argue the question there was a relationship. There was no question Stephanie caught it because he got a look that was both acknowledgment and uncertainty.

"I feel confident you could handle it however many children come along." She found her usual composure and sat down.

"I'm pretty focused on number one right now."

"You do remember I said I wasn't asking you for anything but—"

"Great sex?" He supplied with a grin.

She laughed. "You have delivered there."

He sobered. "Please know I think my dad is the greatest guy on this planet. Should this happen, I want to be part of our child's life however it works out."

"That's fair enough," she said softly, meeting his eyes. "No objection."

"This isn't a courtroom."

"I wasn't speaking as a lawyer, but as a woman."

"I was kind of hoping that was the case."

She settled her napkin on her lap. "The steaks look and smell amazing."

Subject changed — he was fine with that. He had said what he needed to say.

They ate and talked and listened to the weather outside start to get serious and avoided all discussion of the case. It wasn't until they'd essentially finished and he'd refilled her wine glass that Stephanie gazed at him and asked frankly, "Okay, why didn't you remove that tracking device?"

A reasonable question.

"It's obviously magnetic, so I could, it's up to you, but the real question is why does she even want to track you? So she doesn't get caught following you around? I'm stuck on the motive for this. I'm starting to think maybe this does have something to do with Daniel, and in that case, since you aren't seeing him, she'll just go away, but if you remove it, she'll stick around."

She thought about it, but admitted, "He did text me again today. Said he wanted to talk, and it isn't happening. There's absolutely nothing to say. I do not understand his interest after quite a long time of us living our separate lives, but that's his problem. Let's not talk about how he acted the last time we saw each other."

Trey understood his interest full well. "It seems to me maybe he's just not over the split."

"He's not deep enough for that." Her response was derisive. "He's maybe not over the rejection part of it, but that would be ego, not his tender feelings. I know him."

"Alright, I'm going to accept you have a better perception than I do, but let's ask Bailey and Carter before we do anything."

He had some knowledge she didn't have — Senator Grayson was involved in the case. If it wasn't her former boyfriend causing the surveillance, it could have something to do with the murders, and it made him uneasy to tip their hand that they knew she was being followed.

"I guess that makes sense. This is not a problem I have ever encountered before because I am entirely aware I don't have all the information I probably should have." Her elbows were set on the table, her tone combative.

"It doesn't affect your prosecution."

"I'm just supposed to take your word for that?"

He couldn't help it, he gave her a challenging look right back. "Yes. I know what's at stake."

"I don't have much choice now, do I?"

It wasn't a decision to end a possible argument, it was more that she looked very attractive with her hair framing

111

her face in a casual fall and that the sound of the wind and rain instinctively made bed sound good, plus he'd be up early working. Trey simply stood and took two steps to pick her up in his arms, just scooping her up from her chair. "Can we finish this discussion upstairs?"

"In your bedroom? You're going to carry me up there?"

"Yes."

It did end the conflict since she started laughing. "Talk about romance novels. We have to clean this up. No way can we just leave our dinner plates here."

"I'll get it tomorrow."

"No. I agree to end the discussion, but we will clean this up now and like two adults go to bed and forget about the contention and—"

He kissed her.

With intensity and purpose.

Maybe they weren't in court, but he won this particular argument.

Her fingers sifted through his hair and he sensed victory.

Done deal.

He'd clean up the kitchen in the morning.

CHAPTER FOURTEEN

Cold night, inside and out.

So charges had been officially filed. I should be triumphant, but instead feel oddly hollow, like maybe I'd won a war but never engaged in battle.

The lonely warrior. That's been me my whole life.

I've never even known what I was fighting for in the first place.

* * *

The river moved in a slow meander of deep water and he sat and listened to it go by, drinking his coffee and thinking about life in general. Chris was of the opinion the peaks and valleys were just unavoidable, and so being notified by the FBI that he was moving forward in the process of potentially becoming a field agent held only a cautious anticipation of success.

In the meantime, he still had a pretty challenging case to solve.

The positive was he had fingerprints now. It would have made his life a lot easier if there had been a hit through the system, but that was a bust, so whoever owned that gun did not have a criminal record.

However, if he could find a solid suspect, he could match the prints and it would be basically over.

So this was not any kind of career criminal but someone still able to gain access to a gun with filed off serial numbers that would identify it. Certainly not very self-possessed to leave it in the hallway, so the culprit was an impulsive killer and certainly Colin's comments about possible past frightening behavior was an interesting twist.

A brilliant red leaf fluttered down and landed on his leg and Chris absently brushed it off, the breeze cool as he pondered the information. It had rained hard last night and there was a tapestry of colorful leaves all over the ground.

He was pretty decent with cold cases. That was actually what he wanted to do for federal law enforcement. Dissect and put to rest old crimes that had never been resolved. Justice personified.

Right at this moment, he was just glad that Anna Hernandez and Colin's father had agreed he'd be a good choice to take the kid in as they waited for a trial date. In the meantime, Colin needed to be in school because he was due to graduate in the spring and that was even more incentive to wrap up this case before it ever went to a formal trial. He really needed a chance at life.

No pressure.

Chris called Carter, who didn't sound too appreciative when he answered. "It's six thirty in the morning, Bailey."

"Is it?" He hadn't even checked. The wind had finally died down, the back porch was quiet and he'd needed to think.

"Don't you sleep?"

"Not that much. Listen, I've been really bothered about something."

"Three people shot while sleeping in their beds? Huh, go figure, me too. That is bothersome."

Okay maybe he deserved that sarcasm since he'd obviously woken the man from a sound sleep, which he was sorry about. "Apologize to your wife for me for the early call. Look, do you remember that multiple stabbing about three years ago in Willamette that is just sitting there in a file, unsolved."

"Yes." There was an exhale on the other end of the line. "Give me a minute to wake up and follow the thread. I hate to admit it but I'm not thirty-something like you. Older couple, right? Where are you headed with this?"

"It wasn't a shooting, but that person stabbed them in their bed and left the knife in the hallway."

"You know, Bailey, I need to be more awake for this . . . but yes, I certainly remember. You think for some reason it is connected?"

"It is similar enough we need to look at it."

There was a pause. "I agree."

"Surely there are prints on record for the knife."

"If nothing else, we'd have the knife still in evidence since it is an unsolved case."

"What if those prints match?"

"I'm waking up now." Carter's voice was sharper. "That's easy enough. Why do you think this?"

"I feel it."

"At the risk of sounding redundant, because I've mentioned this before, police work doesn't operate that way. Oh Your Honor, I *feel* like the accused is guilty of the crime. A lawyer would not win on that one."

Chris had to ignore the sarcasm. "I get it, but I do sense a link. The impulse and the way it was done. This is it, this is our lead. Finally I'm getting a sense of this. I've been waiting for it."

"You've been waiting for it. What? Like getting sprinkled with magic fairy dust or something."

"I don't know that you and I are the same kind of a cop."

"I've never thought we were. Fine, I trust your instincts. Let's look into it."

He ended the call and listened to a flock of Canada geese pass overhead, heading south and flying so low he could hear the swish of their beating wings.

Anna Hernandez had stayed relatively late, mostly due to making sure she wasn't impaired by that one stiff drink so she could safely drive home, but also because they'd just talked. At first, of course, Colin's predicament had been the topic at hand, but then they'd slipped rather surprisingly into more personal conversation. She told him she'd gone to undergrad at Vanderbilt, and then later decided on graduate school for her master's degree, and in turn he'd told her how he'd done his four years at U of T in Knoxville and walked away with a degree in political science, but decided maybe he was interested in law enforcement.

It was, under unusual circumstances certainly, a little like a first date. A tentative get-to-know-you conversation. Unquestionably she was very attractive, and he found her interesting enough he was sitting there thinking about her at six thirty in the morning over a half empty cup of coffee.

Only briefly did she mention her marriage.

"My mistake," she'd said not bitterly, but there was an edge in her voice, "to marry a man I sensed was in love with someone else."

He didn't ask for details because that was hardly any of his business.

In return, he'd offered: "My last relationship ended because I'm too involved in my job. I just came home one day and it was a done deal. She was moved out and just stayed long enough to make the announcement before she walked out the door. She did leave the dog, so I'm not entirely on my own."

She'd laughed and remarked pragmatically, "Relationships are complicated, there's no denying it."

They were. Chris couldn't help but wonder if Senator Grayson would just man up and tell his wife about Colin. He seemed to genuinely want to help, and while she might not realize regular payments were being made, surely she'd find out about the bail. That was quite a chunk of change. Certainly to a spouse you'd have to justify taking out a withdrawal like that and explain it, but who knew. As a police officer for a county

116

sheriff's department, he thought it was a lot of money, but maybe for the Graysons it wasn't a notable sum.

It would be very interesting to learn how the first meeting between father and son went. Anna had promised him that when she knew Colin was going to be released, she'd let him know.

In the meantime, he'd pursue that cold case and see if he could make a connection. People murdered in their sleep, weapon left in the hallway.

There had to be one.

* * *

She didn't really want to do this.

Rephrase, she *knew* she didn't want to do this.

Anna walked out with Colin, his silence not telling her much. She had keys to the Gaines's house and had gone there to get him street clothes. It felt like a crime scene, dead silent, and there was no question that she was an interloper in his bedroom, opening drawers and picking out some jeans and several nice shirts so he could have his pick — after all he was about to meet his father for the first time.

There was no question she didn't want him to have to go into that house by himself, so she took him to her condo. She'd bought it after the divorce and it suited her needs just fine. No lawn to mow, but a nice patio out back, and the finishes suited her taste, so she liked it. She directed him to the spare bedroom. "There's a bathroom right off of it, so if you want to shower or anything, I'll be downstairs. We have a meeting this afternoon after lunch."

"Okay." He took the bag and never asked who had made bail for him. "Am I going to be staying here with you then?"

"No. You really have someone in your corner. Detective Bailey offered to have you stay with him. Are you fine with that?"

To her relief, he finally showed some emotion. Colin nodded and actually smiled. "Yeah. He's pretty cool."

She thought so too.

He went upstairs and she just ordered a pizza for lunch because she assumed any teenage boy would be good with it. When he came back downstairs he looked more relaxed, was dressed neatly, and had shaved, so looked clean-cut and more like the track athlete colleges might consider for a sports scholarship.

Except those multiple murder charges really might stand in his way.

The pizza was a good call, since he ate like a young man his age would, and she certainly expected the food he'd been fed recently was not top-notch.

When they were done he politely helped clear the plates.

She pointed back at the seat he'd vacated at her kitchen table. "Let's sit down again for a conversation, can we?"

There was no doubt about it, she was used to talking with kids that had troubles, that was her job, but his troubles were not the norm. She chose her words carefully, taking a glance at the whimsical chicken clock on the wall her mother had given her for Christmas. "I just want to prepare you that in a few minutes, your father will be here."

He stared at her in complete consternation. "My . . . *what?*"

"That is who is meeting with us."

"Joe is dead."

She had sympathy because there was no doubt he'd been through quite a bit, but she said firmly, "I understand completely he was who raised you from when you were six and you think of him that way, but I mean your real father. I want to clarify as best I can before he gets here that he was always in the picture. That's why we are talking about this."

"How?" Colin just sat back and shook his head. "I've never even met him."

"He's always paid your mother child support and he's the person that just bailed you out of jail. He's kept track of what you're doing, and he hired you a very competent and expensive lawyer. He cares."

"Then why—"

"He's an important man and don't make me ask if you know how someone intelligent can be careless and get someone pregnant when it isn't the best decision in the world."

"Oh . . . shit. Bailey told you." He shut his eyes and sighed.

"He *has* to tell me. At this moment, I'm responsible for you. And you know what, I'll step in for your child and girlfriend too if it becomes necessary. So, do me a favor and talk to your father from an angle that includes an openness to acknowledge he's here because he's concerned for you."

It took a moment, but he finally lifted his shoulders. "I just didn't know that he ever thought about me."

That statement just broke her heart. She searched for the right words. "From what I understand your parents agreed to these terms and it seems to me, they were content with the situation, but when you got into trouble, your father was paying attention and stepped up. Give him a chance, please?"

"Alright." A bare nod.

"Good decision."

It took him a moment and he finally gave a shrug that was meant to be negligent in a teenaged way, but she knew wasn't. "I didn't know what to do but this."

This was exactly why she had chosen to do this for a living. She looked at him. "Get yourself charged for murder? You are lucky a lot of people don't believe for a minute you did it and care enough to find out who did."

"I *didn't* do it."

"You know I think Bailey might really figure this out."

"He said he wouldn't do anything without talking to me first."

"There's part of your answer right there."

There was a knock on the door.

She said, "I think this might be zero hour. You fine? Colin, I bet he's as nervous as you, if not more."

"Why should *he* be nervous?"

119

Young men were so ingenuous. "You don't think he wouldn't want you to like him? I can tell you he does. Let me get the door."

* * *

Anna's condo was neat and small and in a nice neighborhood.

What Chris expected from a professional woman who seemed to view life through a clear lens. Leather couch, patterned rug in geometrics, some framed photographs on the wall, all comfortable and stylish but no girlish frills. Warm but not too over the top.

It lived up to her straightforward personality.

Colin was in the kitchen and he came out slowly, and honestly, there was no way Chris could blame him for the hesitancy. What an odd take on life to meet your parent when you are seventeen years old. He said warily, "Hi, Detective Bailey."

It was Anna who introduced them. "Colin, this is someone I think you've wanted to meet for a while and the detective and I are going to go out back for a few minutes while you two converse, okay?"

Senator Grayson just looked at his tall son and seemed unable to speak.

To his credit, it was Colin who said, "Are you really my dad?"

Anna touched Chris's arm. "This way."

He followed her through a tidy kitchen to a set of sliding glass doors that led to a small patio with two chairs and a table, a couple of pots of mums giving a splash of color. She said, "I just think it might go better without an audience, don't you? Men are so reluctant to show emotion."

"I'm going to trust your judgment, but no doubt you're right. We feel it but we just aren't geared toward expressing it very well."

Her smile was wry and she chose a chair and sat down, crossing her legs, which were nice and shapely. "At least you admit it."

120

"Unless we are watching a sporting event. Then we tend to express ourselves without any problem. Ever been to a football game?"

"Unfortunately, yes. It isn't my thing."

"What is your thing?" He chose to just lean against the railing.

"A nice jazz bar and a cosmopolitan on the table in front of me. Preferably a vanilla apple mix."

He made a mental note, because he was starting to think they might be trending toward a date, at least once this was all settled. "I'll keep it in mind. Listen, I think already I can give Trey Austin a defense for Colin that would amount to reasonable doubt. My problem is I don't understand quite yet what's going on. I need a sum of the parts, not just a partial equation."

"Oh, and you have never had cryptic slung your way before?" Her dark eyes held an accusing look. "Can you clarify that for me?"

"Not really. I don't have all the facts yet. It's simple enough."

"Nothing about you is simple." Her glossy dark hair brushed her neck as she shook her head. "I seem to have a thing for edgy men."

She had a thing for him? That was some positive news.

Amused, he asked, "Edgy and cryptic? Hmm, what does the psychologist think?"

"Maybe your potty training didn't go well?"

He had to laugh. "That's always possible. I believe I was too young to remember the whole thing."

"You asked. Not to change the subject, but can you give me at least a daily text about how Colin is doing? I've arranged it so he can catch up on his schoolwork online and go forward that way until we have a trial date, which I am hoping won't happen."

It was a sobering thought but yes, it was probably better to not send a kid who was charged with murder back to the public school system. Chris agreed. "Yes."

"He has an ankle monitor and once you have him at your house, it has to be activated."

"I know how it works."

She did smile apologetically then. "Yeah, I know you do, but I have to go through this since I'm not looking at you like a police officer right now, but as a custodial guardian."

"No problem."

"I appreciate this. I pushed through the paperwork because I do think this is a perfect solution and no one disagreed. I'm not sure where he would go otherwise. If his uncle was in the country and able to handle this, it would be different. I did get Colin some clothes, but if he needs anything else, I have keys to the house I'll just give to you."

"His phone?"

"He had it in his car when he was arrested. You'll have to handle that."

"Will do." It was probably still in evidence, so that was no problem.

"Before all of this, he was really at the top of his class. Can we possibly keep him there?"

"I promise to encourage him in that direction." He considered her. "So, when this is over, what happens? He'll be old enough to be on his own in a few months but still in high school. Is there a mortgage on the house? If so, he can't pay it."

"His uncle will. He told me so. My problem is communicating with him is a dicey thing depending on where the aircraft carrier is since he's a naval officer. Email works best, and time zones are an issue, and so far my responsibility really is just Colin's welfare. That sort of thing has to be hashed out by him and attorneys because I have no idea if there's a will or not."

"I assume his defense attorney could get that information."

"Not Trey's area of expertise or what he was hired to do and it would be too much to ask of Colin to expect him to know about his parents' finances."

"I'll find out."

"That's right, you are a detective." The corner of her mouth lifted.

"It opens doors. I assume Colin's uncle would appreciate it if I could get all that sorted out since he can't do it from halfway across the world. I'll get his contact information if you don't mind and make sure he gets copied on anything I find."

"That's a good idea and let me go get those keys."

CHAPTER FIFTEEN

At times I do get introspective, though I try to avoid it.

Freedom is a fluid concept, I've decided.

It all depends on your personal definition of what confines you, traps you against your will and holds you hostage.

It can be physical, or it certainly can be mental.

I am not sure which one is worse.

* * *

A call from Anna was not necessarily welcome at any time, but this wasn't personal, so after answering it cautiously he relaxed.

"Your client is currently in the care of Detective Bailey to the extent he is his temporary guardian. He offered and it was approved."

Short and sweet.

"It does seem like a good solution. How did the visit with his father go?"

"Feel free to ask him or the senator."

End of call. No goodbye, she just hung up.

The tenuous state of their civility would probably unravel completely if she found out he was involved with Stephanie, but certainly he still had his own life to live. She was allowed to be ticked off at him because feelings were what they were, but he was also allowed to ignore the hostility, some of which he maybe deserved, and some that he did not.

He and Stephanie had not yet discussed what she'd tell everyone if she did get pregnant. He'd entered into the agreement on a purely emotional level and who knew if it was a mistake, but he'd done it, and so it went.

There was no way he'd take back the night before. Midnight whispers, the feel of her in the dark with the keening wind outside, the erotic pleasure and closeness. She was right, it probably was like a romance novel, but maybe that was exactly what it was supposed to be like.

Wasn't it?

He had no idea, he was still on a learning curve, so what he did concentrate on was a short text from Chris Bailey.

I have matching prints from the weapon that killed Joe Gaines, Roxanne, and her mother from another multiple homicide. They aren't Colin's.

Trey sat there, registering the implication.

Huge.

He texted back: *Can we meet to discuss this?*

I think that's a good idea but you'll have to come to me. I have this river cabin and Colin and I are headed out there now. Ms. St. James knows where it is if you want to invite her to sit in.

She had told him that much but no other explanation. He was still curious.

He called her but just got her voicemail. Truthfully, they really didn't account to each other for their schedules, but seemed to be taking it one day at a time. In one way, it was perfect, but neither was it a real commitment.

Except a child together would definitely be a permanent connection.

She called back twenty minutes later and seemed harried, but interested in the information and a meeting. "Our office is of course interested in prosecuting a multiple offender, especially if it involves homicides. That goes without saying."

"Multiple homicides or so it appears."

"That is pretty interesting."

"I need to talk to Bailey anyway. Anna was not forthcoming about much." She couldn't see his humorless smile over the phone. "Our conversations are short and terse. Bailey is apparently at this time in charge of Colin. He said they are at his cabin and since you've been there, you know the way."

"I do. Give me a time. I'll pick you up at your office?"

"I just have paperwork left for today. You can come anytime."

"Give me an hour."

"I'll let him know."

True to her word she was right on time. He slid into the car after she called him from the parking lot, definitely much more used to being the one driving and amused at his adolescent reaction to having her pick him up instead of the other way around.

"If this was a date—"

"Masculinity issues because *I* just picked *you* up?" There was amusement in her voice at her accurate guess. "Look at it this way, you don't seem to have performance issues."

"I feel better now." He laughed and shook his head. "Can we talk about the information Bailey imparted instead? So now it looks like I can present a pretty solid defense it is someone else."

"You know for a fact I don't want to take this case to court. I want to hear what he has to say. Plus, if Colin was so adamant charges be pressed, he has the answer. I'm frustrated all the way around. He could walk free if he would just talk."

"He did give over the murder weapon."

She glanced over, driving competently on the winding roads. "As an observer from the outside, he's trying to help us but mired up in something else. What's he so afraid of?"

"Maybe Bailey can answer that question for us both. I know pretty much what you know."

"Trey, if there are unsolved cases connected to this, who knows what evidence he could give us."

"I'm starting to get a pretty good sense of Detective Bailey. He'd love to hand over those cases to you with solid evidence. Why else would a single thirty-one-year-old man volunteer to take on a teenager charged with murder? It's for a short time, but still, he's busy, young enough to have a social life, and yet there's no doubt he volunteered. Which is probably a good thing, since who the heck else would do it on the chance Colin is guilty."

After a moment, she did acquiesce. "I'm going to admit that makes sense to me. Bailey seems like a decent man with a purpose and a sharp investigator. Maybe Colin will confide in him if they spend more time together."

"I'm going to guess that's what he's hoping will happen."

"Guessing doesn't work in police work, does it?"

"Not for a lawyer, but this is a discussion, not in court."

"True enough, I'll concede that point. Did he say who the other victims might be?"

"On the phone, no. Face to face is going to be the key here which is why we are driving . . . where? To a river cabin to talk to him instead of me maybe taking you out to a nice Italian restaurant and having us drink Chianti and gaze into each other's eyes."

"Was that the plan?"

"Something like that."

"Ah, the date reference. Then you should definitely have picked me up instead of the other way around." Her mouth twitched into a smile.

"I'll get over it. It isn't exactly like we have a particularly traditional path to a relationship anyway."

"Oh, I assume you are referencing me asking you to donate sperm to my cause."

He looked at her, the late-afternoon sunlight touching her hair through the windows of the car, and asked, "And what did you make of my immediate agreement and request that we follow along the lines of nature instead of science?"

"What did you make of my comment that I was hoping you'd lean that direction?"

"Answering a question with a question?" He had to counter.

"Avoiding it?"

He had to answer, because it was a legitimate argument. He said truthfully, "I think that was one of the best moments of my life."

* * *

When she'd been there before it had been late, and she'd departed early on a gray day. On a nice evening she thought the cabin was charming in a weathered sort of way, no pretention to anything but what it was, an old structure built near a scenic stream, surrounded thickly by trees, the soft sound of moving water in the background.

Autumn leaves drifted down in a colorful fall and the air smelled clean and cool. There was smoke coming from the chimney and a truck in the driveway instead of the black car.

"This is it."

"I think rustic does apply." Trey opened his door and he was definitely overdressed in tailored slacks and a nice shirt, but he'd lost his tie on the way and it was slung into the back seat of her car, his shirt partially unbuttoned at the neck, and his raven hair stylishly just a little unruly.

Her level of involvement was pretty high.

His physical attraction wasn't in question, she didn't think anyone would argue that point, but he was also intelligent, considerate, and had a sense of humor, three attributes she valued.

She also got out, the sunset casting a reddish hue over the sky.

"Nice to be able to get away and be by yourself, especially if you have Bailey's job," she commented.

"Or ours," Trey agreed dryly. "Though he sees the grimmer side of crime, and we just hash out the punishment. Let's go see what he has to say."

The person that opened the door was Colin and he was holding a bottle of light beer. "Hi. Come on in. Okay, Bailey said I could have just one. Joe used to let me once in a while."

Stephanie said, "I don't think either I or Trey care one way or the other. We aren't here for that. You okay?"

"Well, I'm out of jail and drinking a beer at a pretty cool cabin. I'm good."

The place was as she remembered it and she could see how a teenaged boy would think it was cool. Masculine with no frills, nothing but the basics of a comfortable couch, a coffee table that had seen better days, and a very plain pine kitchen table with several ladder-backed chairs.

So the little dog that embraced their entrance was a little out of place. A long-haired bundle of joyous welcome of someone who she obviously recognized as a friend and greeted her with a warm pink tongue and a wagging tail. "This is the moppet," she told Trey, bending to stroke the dog's silky head. "I assume she has a real name but I don't know it."

"That's Bailey's dog?" He looked amused, but she hadn't really believed it either. "I think I expected a German Shepherd or maybe some kind of hunting breed."

"His girlfriend decamped but didn't take her dog."

"I see."

"He'll be back in a minute. He went to get some more firewood." Colin supplied the information looking at them curiously. "Uhm, can I ask? Why are you both here? He said you were coming, but nothing else."

She straightened. "I think I'm going to let him handle this. You wanted to be charged with murder, which is a first for me because no one wants that. Now he seems to be on the track of another murder that has nothing to do with you but might be linked to what happened to your family. We all need to sit and talk, but I know no details at all."

"I'm here to listen in. Your father wants your rights properly represented." Trey said it with calm inflection.

"This way, I can know exactly what was said and who said it. That's my role."

"You came together?"

Stephanie had to give him credit for maybe being a little confused. "Trey and I are hardly enemies just because we represent a different side of the cases we handle. We've known each other for quite a while and are friends."

With benefits, as the saying went. She left out that part, but somehow she thought Colin might have caught on anyway from the sudden reassessment in his gaze as he looked from one of them to the other. "Oh."

Bright kid.

Damn.

She hoped not everyone could figure it out so easily.

Luckily, Chris Bailey came in then, carrying some logs he deposited by the woodstove. "Mr. Austin, Ms. St. James. Something to drink while we sit down and talk? I believe I have beer, water and coffee, and yes, I know Colin shouldn't be drinking underage, but you know, I'm afraid I did it in my long past youth, so I agreed to just one."

It wasn't like the irony of it all escaped her and Stephanie said wryly, "Nothing for me. I'm driving."

"I'll take a beer, since I'm not." Trey shrugged and gave her an amused look, but he didn't really realize the circumstances under which she'd met Bailey in the first place, so she just went for a bland expression.

Someday maybe she'd tell him it was due to seeing him at that reception with the brunette on his arm, making her drink at least one or two glasses of wine too many, but they weren't there yet. Lovers, yes, but just because of her unusual request? The exchange in the car on their way here made her wonder, and he *had* agreed pretty much immediately . . . but they definitely had an interesting past.

"Have a seat, please, so we can have a conversation." Bailey motioned to the simple table and looked pointedly at Colin. "You get to be part of this. You can just listen, or you can chime in if you have something to say."

He opened the refrigerator and took out two beers, handed one to Trey and twisted the cap off the other and sat down.

"So, three years ago," he began in a conversational tone, "someone went into the house of Carol and Mark McConnell and stabbed them both with a butcher knife while they were sleeping, and left the knife in the hallway. No sign of forced entry and the fingerprints on the knife match those also on the gun used in the murders of the Gaines family. Now we are talking five murders. I need a connection."

Now she understood why she and Trey were there. He needed to question Colin and still needed vindication it was not done under duress with his attorney present and with her as a witness as well, so it would definitely fly in court.

"I remember that case," she said thoughtfully. "No viable suspects. Then it went cold."

"Until now. It is no longer under chill factor." Bailey looked at Colin. "If you can help me connect the dots I sure would appreciate it."

CHAPTER SIXTEEN

*"Desperate, proud, fond, sick, accepted by men,
rejected by men,
They go! They go! I know that they go, but I know
not where they go."*

*Yes, I read poetry now and then and Walt Whitman is a favorite
for some reason.*
I believe it is his frank take on immortality in Leaves of Grass.
My grandfather gave me a battered copy of the book and I kept it.
For some reason that passage has always stuck out.
I believe he is talking about death, but that might just be me.

* * *

If anyone thought Chris would want to spend an evening at
the cabin with a district attorney and a defense lawyer, not
to mention someone charged with murder, the answer would
normally be no thank you. He went there to relax usually and
forget his job.

Not tonight.

The moppet appeared to be enamored of his guests,
especially Stephanie St. James who she'd met before. He did

wonder if the little dog missed Sara, but he couldn't do a damn thing about that.

Failed love affair. A story as old as the ages.

But she'd left him because Chris knew he was a focused individual, and at the moment, he was very focused, so she'd have a legitimate complaint.

"Do the names mean anything to you?"

Colin just looked at him and shrugged helplessly. "No."

He thought the kid was telling the truth, so he tried again. "You said someone 'really messed up' committed the crime. What did that mean?"

"You know, I've met a lot of people in my life, and I assess whether or not I like them, and I like your dad." That was Austin weighing in. "I think he's worried, and I think he hates what happened to your mom. If you want my opinion, that is it. If you can help, do it for him and for her, Joe, and your grandmother."

"I have just my own idea of who it could be because this person is crazy enough it *could* be them. That's all I have." Colin actually looked a little pale and he stared down at the beer can sitting in front of him rather than look at anyone else. "I think that when this person went into our house that night, they were looking for me and when I wasn't there, they just killed everyone who was there."

That accounted for his remark that he had managed to get his entire family killed, Chris thought grimly.

"Is this drug-related in any way?" He had to ask it.

That brought Colin's head up. "What? No."

"He tested clean after he was taken into custody." Trey said, "He volunteered to do it."

"Just because you sell drugs, does not mean you take them. It's a legitimate question." Stephanie backed him up. "Those people are ruthless. I've prosecuted a few dealers and violent crime goes hand in hand with their chosen profession."

"It has nothing to do with drugs." Colin was emphatic. "I don't take them, buy them, or sell them. I've tried weed like twice but didn't really like it. I want to run collegiate track."

Want. That word hung in the air. The way things stood, he just had a dream and a desire. Now he was charged with three counts of murder and had a pregnant girlfriend.

Chris had to struggle with not making an absolute promise because nothing in this world was a given, but if he just had something so he could solve these cases, maybe the dream could come true.

He considered his words carefully. "So let's make sure I understand exactly where we are. You do not know anything about the older couple that was killed, correct?"

"No, not correct."

Austin leaned forward. "Colin, please, if you can help, now is the time. Talking in circles doesn't help Detective Bailey and we are discussing a second homicide investigation. That means a second grieving family with no answers. It will help everyone, and especially you, if you would just be forthcoming with what you do know."

"I didn't know their names, but I knew something bad like that had happened."

"How?"

"My girlfriend told me she knew someone who had killed two people and that this person might come after me. I can put two and two together."

"Can I talk to her?"

"No. If you did, she might get killed too. You promised you wouldn't do anything without talking to me first."

Chris kept his tone calm. "I *am* talking to you."

"I know." Colin faltered and muttered, "I'm pretty scared about all of this in case no one has noticed."

Stephanie St. James said definitively, "We've noticed. We're scared too. So just to clarify for me, your plan is that this person will relax if they think you're going down for their crime and your girlfriend will be safer because they won't be so worried about being caught. They also will have revenge for whatever it is you did to send them over the edge?"

134

Smart question. Chris was really interested in the answer. "Yeah."

Chris said, "So, if I can figure this out, get enough to make an arrest so this person is off the street, and Ms. St. James can get charges pressed, we would all be happier?"

"I suppose."

"I'm not saying I'm a topnotch sleuth or anything, but give me a clue, and I still give you my word I'll talk to you first before I approach anyone. Colin, the last thing I want is for anyone else to be hurt. That is not my job, just the opposite."

"I don't know what to do." He put his head in his hands.

"Is this connected to your girlfriend no one really knows anything about? Angry father? She's pregnant and you are responsible and he's super ticked off?"

"That's leading a witness."

Chris sent Trey Austin a look for that intervention. "Does this look like a court of law to you? There are deer antlers holding rifles above the door and we are drinking beer. I'm just asking after making an educated guess."

Austin looked right back. "I want you to ask him the right questions. Your theories of what might be happening are fine, but in my line of work, they are considered speculation, and he's seventeen. You are right, antlers and all, but you wanted Steph and me here for a reason."

He had a point. "There's a connection and I need it."

"No. Not her father." Colin was steady and just shook his head. "I promise you. He's not in the picture anymore."

First clue.

"Divorce?"

"Yes."

"What else will you tell me?"

"Just that I know she's killed other people." He stood. "Do you mind if I take the moppet down to the river before it gets too dark while I finish my beer? It's a nice night."

Chris just lifted his shoulders. "Nope, don't mind at all."

After he left, the dog following with enthusiasm, all three of them looked at each other.

It was Stephanie that said, "She?"

"I'm looking for a single mom apparently. I got something out of that conversation anyway."

"A knife is not typically a woman's weapon," Trey pointed out.

"No," Chris agreed. "But those prints match and it does happen sometimes."

"It could still be the father," Stephanie pointed out. "Maybe he isn't voluntarily out of the picture."

"I guess I need to talk to his friends again. See if any of them can give me a sense of who his girlfriend might be."

Stephanie offered a suggestion. "Ask Anna Hernandez if she'll do it. She's great with kids and not a cop, not a lawyer, or a district attorney. She might have more success."

That actually was not a bad idea.

And he'd get to see her again.

He walked them to their car, the crisp fall breeze carrying wood smoke and the earthy scent of damp earth.

Austin said, "One more thing. I have something for you and a favor to ask. Can you have this checked for prints and if you find one run it through your database?"

What he handed over in a plastic bag was a surprise. Chris looked at it and glanced up. "A tracking device?"

"Someone seems to be following Stephanie. Her neighbor saw someone put it on her car. We debated taking it off or not and finally decided to remove it. The neighbor took a picture of the woman and Steph has no idea who she might be."

They'd both been very cooperative and he didn't like the idea ever of someone following a district attorney around. There could be a vendetta involved and he liked Stephanie St. James. He promised, "I will look into it, no problem. Send me the picture too."

* * *

It was a quiet drive back to Willamette, probably both he and Stephanie contemplating the implications of what they'd learned and what was at stake.

All the way around.

One thing Trey now knew was the fact the murderer was most likely female, and for some reason that could maybe have nothing do with this case — he had to acknowledge that — a strange woman was shadowing Stephanie.

Unsettled didn't even describe his reaction to that information.

Finally she spoke. "So, do you view that particular interaction as worth it?"

"I think my view is does Bailey view it as worth it? I think he got something out of it and did it in a way that could be clearly seen as he never questioned Colin with any duress involved. We all consider the circumstances to be pretty unusual."

"Oh, you mean the detective investigating three murders taking in the suspect charged with the crimes as a foster parent? Yes, unusual applies."

"It makes pretty good sense, though I suspect Anna had to pull some strings to let that happen." He didn't really want to talk about his ex-wife and so he focused on the evening ahead. "Pick up some Chinese and my house again?"

"I need to go home and change."

Since he was still dressed for work as well, he understood. "We'll stop there first then."

"I'll drop you at the office because your car is there."

"No. I like keeping you in my line of vision. Great scenery. Let me enjoy."

She glanced over. "Nice deflection."

"I highly doubt I'm charming, but I try now and then."

"Takeout food sounds fine. It's been a long day." Her smile reflected her unrest. "I agree with you that hopefully Colin will continue to at least help Bailey out with some persuasion. I think it isn't at all he doesn't want to talk, he's just afraid to talk."

"Your summary was about right. If it looks like he's going to prison for it, mission accomplished by the real killer. They've still taken his life and walked away free and clear."

"Taken his family." Stephanie said the words with clear sympathy. "Except now, he's not going to prison, for which I am so relieved. In court you'd shred our case with the print comparison, so if Bailey can work some more of his investigative magic — and I'm really starting to think he can — we'll just drop the charges."

She was right. If prints from a previous murder with a similar scenario were at both scenes, his defense was pretty rock solid now where before he was standing on quicksand.

Except there was another issue. Trey told her, "Until Bailey checks that tracking device for a viable print, I believe you and I are going to spend a lot of time together."

For that declaration he got a sidelong glance. "I'm aware and alert."

"I thought that was the plan anyway. The time together thing."

"I'm not objecting to that necessarily, but you don't have to protect me."

"Has it occurred to you I might want to do just that?"

"Alpha male syndrome?"

"Or is it perhaps someone concerned that a person is stalking you and does not want any harm to come to you?"

Because they just might be in love with you.

He wasn't ready to say it because he was pretty sure she wasn't ready to hear it.

He'd settle for the arrangement they had right now.

"I admit I'm curious too, but I really think getting a print is unlikely."

He followed the logic and agreed. "I'm wondering if it might be a private investigator hired either by Daniel himself to see if you are involved with anyone, or a lover who has found out he's contacting you again. If it is, a print is very unlikely. They would use gloves."

"I admit the timing is suspicious. He starts sending me messages and suddenly someone is trying to keep track of me? But why bother? I truly have not seen him, even just an accidental encounter in a grocery store aisle or putting gas in my car, or some similar scenario, in several years."

"He might wonder if you are seeing someone if he wants to, as they say, rekindle that old flame, which it seems to me he does."

"Would you hire someone to follow Anna around?"

"No. Then again, I don't think he and I have much in common except for an interest in you and I have no desire to get back together with Anna."

He was telling the complete truth there.

"She never did tell me what really happened."

It wasn't like he hadn't known that tentative question might be coming and he knew well why Anna had never said anything to Stephanie about the split.

"She seemed perpetually convinced I was unfaithful and the truth is, no, I wasn't. Not. One. Time." He enunciated the last three words very clearly.

"Oh. I see."

Well, physically he never had been, but emotionally, it was a grayer area. Anna wasn't entirely wrong.

Stephanie turned off the small county highway. "I can see where that might be a real problem and why she might not want to talk about it."

"Yes," he said neutrally. "It was a real problem."

CHAPTER SEVENTEEN

I do to a certain extent regret the death of my parents.
It was a rash decision, and I'm undecided if they deserved it or not.
But to me, that says it all.
Undecided.
Maybe they did.

* * *

The cafeteria was crowded, of course, but a very nice guidance counselor had steered her in the right direction.

There was no question Anna wasn't a detective, but on the other hand, in her profession she did have to question children about personal experiences and make assessments, and so she handled it that way.

When Chris Bailey called her, she'd readily agreed to do this even though her workload was pretty high. She'd take the time to help any child escape a murder trial and possible conviction.

"So Colin just never said anything about having a new girlfriend?" She had sat down at a table with some of the track team jocks and to their credit, though they looked uncomfortable at first, they were all polite enough to listen to her questions.

It had to be disconcerting to have a friend charged with murder.

"No." One of them was fairly tall like Colin, so maybe they ran the same distance in competition. Unruly brown hair, an athletic build, he really seemed to consider her question. "This is Willamette. Not a really big high school. If he had been dating anyone from here, we'd probably know it. There's another high school close by that is consolidated, so that's possible. She could be a country kid."

"But he never mentioned a name or anything?"

"Emily."

Anna's attention sharpened. It was one of the other guys at the table, and he shrugged. "She came to a meet last spring. She's pretty hot and I didn't recognize her but he went up between races and sat with her and they looked . . . I don't know, like they were kind of together. I asked him who she was, and all he told me was 'That's Emily'."

At least she had a first name. "Anything else?"

"I can tell you she doesn't go to our school."

That helped, or she assumed it did. Bailey was going to take whatever information she was able to glean from this venture and then do what he seemed to do best and decipher the mystery.

Maybe she'd tell him over dinner.

It was in the back of her mind, though she thought romance was off her jaded plate, he'd piqued her interest, and she had the understated impression it might be mutual.

"Can you give me a brief description? I realize that was some time ago, but hair color and an idea of her height might be helpful. You said she was 'hot', so maybe you still have a visual?"

"Uh, dark hair. Nice . . . er . . . build . . . whatever you'd call it."

Anna helped him out. "So she's stacked and pretty, right?"

He smiled sheepishly. "Right. Height, like I said, she was sitting in the stands. But he's pretty tall and they were next

141

to each other so I'd say about average for a girl. Definitely shorter than him."

"Thanks, that is helpful."

Or she imagined it might be to the right person, and that was Bailey. To her looking for a teenaged girl with only a first name was like hunting for the proverbial needle in a stack of hay, but he did a far different job than she was qualified to do, so she called him on the way back to her office.

"I have a first name that might be helpful, a description, and found out she doesn't attend the same high school, but there is a consolidated one not too far away, so maybe a possibility she's from a town close by?"

He said, "That's better than I did, so thank you because I think I can figure out the high school without any problem from a phone number connection. Ms. St. James suggested I ask you and apparently she was right."

She didn't want to talk about how Stephanie was as bright as she was beautiful . . . she was really trying to get past it. "No problem. I could give you a more detailed recital of the conversation I had with Colin's friends tonight maybe over dinner? I have to say the recipe my grandmother passed along for her enchiladas is legendary. We can eat and then Colin can watch television or something if he doesn't want to be part of the conversation."

In her life, she'd never asked a man on a date, if this even qualified. She'd always been the one who had been approached. At this moment, she understood how difficult it must be to be an adolescent male stammering out an invitation that might be rejected.

"That sounds like a very good idea. I was wondering if you might have dinner with me anyway one-on-one, but we can definitely mix business with pleasure now that I have a sidekick."

What a relief that she hadn't misread the signals. With Trey, she'd been on the blind side and it had left her very wary of involvement with anyone. "Great." She did a swift calculation of how fast she could throw dinner together. "What, six o'clock?"

"I will see you then."

She hung up and was in a good mood an hour later when her desk phone rang. "Anna Hernandez."

That vanished quickly.

"Did you really get a murderer released from jail?"

She was startled but her office number was public. "I'm sorry, but who are you referring to?"

The call ended.

That was odd, was all she could think of as a reaction. Not necessarily hostile but still disturbing, said in an accusatory tone.

It had to be about Colin making bail, though in truth she had nothing to do with that happening. Certainly she hadn't handled any other cases with a child charged with murder, so it had to be the connection.

It could be anyone calling because, of course, it had made the news Colin had made bail after being charged with three counts of felony murder as an adult and somehow was given the funds by an anonymous donor.

She was suddenly very glad Colin was with Bailey. That his life could be threatened was not in question. People were unpredictable and she'd seen some unfortunate situations. There was no doubt she'd been threatened more than once by angry parents or relatives when she'd recommended the removal of a child from a dangerous environment. Since they were usually the source of the problem in the first place, she took those seriously, but this had just been a vague accusation.

When it came to Colin, he had a law enforcement officer with a weapon at his back, so that was reassuring after that questionable phone call. Why she was being blamed was strange because if anyone thought social services was in the habit of dolling out money to bail out their charges, they would be wrong.

But the senator did want to keep this quiet and she understood it, so there it was.

Maybe this evening she'd get some answers but truthfully, as things stood, it was really up to Trey and Stephanie now to settle the future of this young man in a legal clash, and up to Chris Bailey to clear him of those charges before it came to that battle.

She was just part of the backstory now.

The grocery store was crowded, but she expected it, and she picked up some ground pork and corn tortillas, a few fresh tomatoes, an avocado for guacamole, and she had the homemade red chili sauce done already, so just some extra cheese and she was done.

Easy dinner, not an easy way to get acquainted.

This was not simple with a teenager's life entangled in the middle.

She'd tell Bailey about the call but it wasn't like the caller had said anything significant. No direct threat anyway.

She wondered if Colin would talk about this Emily, or refuse to discuss her, or if Chris Bailey would even want him to know they'd managed to get a name.

Probably not until he looked into it first would be her guess.

It should be an interesting evening and she spent far too many of them alone, so she was looking forward to it.

* * *

There was no question that the enchiladas lived up to the promise, as Chris had never had anything like them down in the hills of Tennessee before and they were fiery hot and delicious. Certainly Colin approved as he devoured them like a starving street urchin. Food was always an afterthought in his preoccupied life, so Chris needed to pay more attention to that.

Anna looked striking in a red blouse that suited her dark coloring, and gray slacks, and her expression reflected amused appreciation as they continued to eat long after she'd finished.

"I'm glad I decided to make a double pan."

"It's really good," Colin said, and added politely, "thank you."

"There's dessert. Have you ever had flan?"

"No."

"Picture caramel and custard."

Chris said, "As a country bumpkin might say, sounds darned tasty to me."

"I'm well aware you have a college degree, Detective, so you can't pull off the bumpkin claim." Anna arched a brow.

"Bumpkins can go to college."

"Is that right? Bumpkin U? Or is it U of B?"

Colin laughed. "You guys are funny." Then his expression went shuttered. "My parents used to talk like that to each other."

It was Anna who knew the right thing to say, since Chris did not.

"Remember them that way. Happy and teasing each other." Her voice was soft. "They would want that for you."

"Yeah, I know my mom would." Colin blinked several times.

Okay, so Chris wasn't perfect at comforting teenaged boys, but maybe he could get them off the hook for murders they didn't commit.

The dessert was delicious, creamy and sweet. Anna revealed her grandmother had grown up in New Mexico — it had a unique cuisine and flan was quite popular.

He was learning small things about her.

After dinner, he helped clear the table and Colin to his credit definitely chipped in, offering to wash the dishes or at least load the dishwasher.

He was starting to like the kid more and more and the motivation to get him out of his current predicament was escalating to major levels. In short, he needed to solve this case as soon as possible, and it wasn't just about him either.

145

The cold case bothered him immensely.

He'd reviewed it in the file multiple times and it was apparent the investigators couldn't find a motive or a clear suspect and besides the prints and no sign of forced entry, no similarities.

Except the weapon left behind in the hallway by the bedroom and that the victims had been asleep.

For him, that was a defiant signature.

Impulsive crimes.

There, I did it. Catch me.

This person didn't have good brakes.

Seriously messed up.

He wasn't going to argue that. To leave the murder weapon with their prints on it? At both scenes?

Granted the crimes were years apart, but give law enforcement some credit. The dots would be connected at some point. He was certainly determined to do it.

When they were finished with at least the basic clean up, he looked at Colin. "Ms. Hernandez and I are going to go have a discussion and you are welcome to join us, or not. I'm sure you already know it is about you, so if I were you, I'd be curious, but if you choose not to do so, fine. I promised you I would talk to you first, and here's your opportunity if you want it."

"Like what?" He didn't look happy. "Something new has happened? I've been with you all the time."

Chris leaned on the marble counter and looked at his new charge. "I need you to tell me about Emily."

Colin tried, but he was never going to be a career criminal because he didn't pull off ignorance. "Who?"

"I am doing something we are never supposed to do in my profession by assuming she might be your girlfriend and you won't say anything for a reason."

That was truly an assumption since he had no evidence that girl in the stands was at all connected to any of what was happening.

"Stay away from her, please." He ran his fingers through his hair and visibly swallowed. "If you showed up to talk to her, I don't know what would happen."

"As of now, I don't know her last name."

Colin looked at him and said hollowly, "But you'll find out."

"I appreciate your confidence in my ability to do so."

Anna finished wiping off the counter and joined the conversation by saying in a calm tone, "Colin, we all understand, as much as we can because we haven't walked that mile in your shoes — you've recently suffered some trauma, and that is difficult for anyone, but it doesn't have to be you against the world. Detective Bailey wants to catch a killer, not endanger Emily."

Truer words never spoken.

"Look, I don't want to accidentally put her in danger in my investigation." Chris aimed for the same measured voice. "But I have to pursue this since five people are dead. There's a very dangerous person out there and I want them off the streets. Just give me something and I promise to not involve Emily if possible."

"That's the problem. You'll have to involve her."

The clouds were breaking in an overcast sky. Finally some light.

"This person is related to her?"

"Yeah."

Chris tried to see if he could get just a little more. "How close?"

The door shut. "I'm going to take the offer of opting for some TV."

Okay, no more information, but he had at least more than he did before. He and Anna watched Colin leave the room, and her only comment was succinct. "This is really difficult."

Chris said dryly, "For both of us."

"He's seventeen."

"I know. It is hard enough to negotiate the turbulent waters of that age without three murder charges and a pregnant girlfriend. Please note I let him just walk away without pushing it."

She looked at him with an inquiring expression on her face. "Why is it I get the impression you are satisfied with what you did get."

"Because I am. I know who I'm hunting now, I just need one more piece of information, and I think I now know how to get it."

CHAPTER EIGHTEEN

Pushing the envelope is my signature ill-fated style and I can't seem to change it.

My luck won't always hold.

I'm well aware.

* * *

"So, I hope you realize the entire office knows you are sleeping with a certain beautiful district attorney."

Trey glanced up from his computer and saw Richard in the doorway, one shoulder against the frame, his pose negligent.

"What?"

"Anonymous tip sent to all the partners along with a picture of her car in your driveway at one in the morning, and then a second one when the sun was coming up. The elegant note said, and I quote: 'Is it ethical for opposing counsel to be fucking each other?'"

He leaned back and contemplated that, wondering over both the graphic crudity and the purpose of it. Dryly, he said, "Funny, I didn't get that memo."

"Is it true?"

If it was anyone else, he would not answer, but at the end of it all, he just said, "Dorset, you've been telling me to ask her out."

"Hey, all I can say is good for you."

"Is it a question of ethics in your mind?"

"Uhm, no. I know you both and you'll do your jobs in a professional manner."

"I agree, but thanks."

Today Richard's tie was a flamboyant sunset with a yacht on an azure sea. He came in and sat down in one of the leather chairs on the opposite side of the desk. "Who did you piss off that would do something like that?"

"Good question. Steph's ex-boyfriend is a frontrunner in my mind, but some strange woman has been following her. I don't know what purpose it would serve anyone to attack either one of us. They went so far as to put a tracking device on her car. The police have it now. We are aware there's a problem."

His friend gave him an appraising look. "Couldn't be Anna?"

No. He didn't think that for a moment and shook his head. "Not her style. When she's ticked off she comes right at you. There's nothing backhanded about her. You always know where you stand. Besides, we're divorced."

"That doesn't mean it is over for her. Does she know about you and Stephanie?"

"I doubt it, that's my point. I would have already gotten an earful and I'm not looking forward to the event when it happens, but she would never do something like that. She's not spiteful, she just speaks her mind."

"I know Anna and I doubt it too. I just tossed it out there. Who would?"

"Suddenly Steph's ex has been contacting her but their split was quite a while ago. I can see him regretting the ruined relationship, but this petty crap is just unlikely from him in my mind. He isn't geared to go to that much effort."

"I'm not surprised you aren't a fan. This woman . . . any clue? District attorneys handle a lot of cases. I'm sure she's made a few enemies because don't we all."

"No clue. But I'm really hoping Bailey comes through with a fingerprint from the tracking device."

"Chris Bailey?"

"Yeah, he is still investigating that triple homicide my client has been charged with and as a matter of fact, Colin Simon is staying with him."

"Is he really?" Richard looked surprised.

"Anna arranged it. When you think about it, the kid would be a hard sell to the average foster parent, but Bailey offered."

"You know, I can always see him walking down a dusty street with his six shooters, ready for a showdown. He can handle a seventeen-year-old boy. I'd love to know how your client made bail, but you aren't going to tell me, so why ask." Richard smiled ironically. "I just thought you should know about the unusual delivery. Why is it I'm going to guess the winsome Ms. St. James's boss got a similar note and those same pictures?"

Hell, Trey hoped not. Stephanie would be extremely unhappy if that was true. He wasn't happy either.

"Did you just use the word 'winsome' in a sentence?"

"I did and I'm kind of proud of it. I always wanted to toss that one out there." Richard got to his feet.

"Thanks for the heads-up. I'm not sure why my personal life needs to be broadcast to the firm and very much object to the way that note was phrased because that hardly describes our relationship, but like I said, we are aware there's some sort of problem."

"It seems like there is. Be careful."

He left and Trey sat there looking at his phone, trying to decide if he should tell Stephanie. It was possible this was aimed at him, though she was the one being followed . . .

It was a hard call.

He was a defense attorney, so all of his clients were charged with crimes or they wouldn't need him. She was a prosecutor, so she charged people with the crimes they committed. Really, it could be anyone related to a case that hadn't gone the way they wanted. An angry family member maybe, so that's why they didn't recognize her?

His phone rang then, and the decision was taken from him when he saw the number. He answered with no real greeting. "Let me guess why you're calling. Someone decided to advertise our relationship to your office?"

"It happened to you, too?"

"It did."

"If this has anything to do with Daniel I apologize."

"Please, Steph, even if it does, it is hardly your fault and if the entire world's population knew we were spending time together, I could care less. I did not like the way it was phrased, but then again, it was obviously malicious."

"If Ed Hanover doesn't pull me off the case, I'd be surprised. He's so conservative it is sometimes hard to work with him, and he's my boss and second counsel. That he's handling this as well might be the only reason I get to go to trial." She added, "I'm hoping that doesn't happen anyway."

"Me too."

"I guess we will see what happens. I'm trying to decide if I should just cave in and talk to Daniel. I don't want to, but if he is seeing someone with vindictive tendencies, or has had a recent break-up and somehow she connects it to me, I'd like to put a stop to it."

"I'm thinking the latter is more probable, and while I understand your reluctance, maybe you should ask him about it and even send him her picture." He paused and then said, "I'd do it for you but he and I never liked each other very much and I doubt he'd talk to me."

"I doubt he would either."

"I'm apparently more transparent than I knew."

"I think we both might be guilty of that." She sighed audibly. "I guess I'll call him since you agree, but to be honest, I'm not certain he'll tell the truth to me either. I don't know what it is he wants in the first place."

We both might be guilty of that.

Despite Robert's unwanted news, his day just got a lot better. "Let me know how it goes and needless to say, don't agree to a face to face."

"No worries there. I don't even want to make the phone call."

* * *

She heard his voice, familiar enough she had a physical reaction to it.

So much for no face to face.

It seemed like while Daniel didn't answer his phone, he got her message she needed to talk to him and came in person to her office.

This day just got better and better. Not.

First having Hanover come to her desk and hand her that note with an inquiring look on his face was not perfect. At all.

All the district attorney asked was, "True?"

Not her finest moment.

"It isn't a conflict of interest and the way it is put is insulting to say the least. You know both me and Trey Austin. He's the most competent defense attorney I know and would always act in the interest of his client, and I would never do anything but follow the letter of the law."

Hanover had actually accepted that and walked away.

Daniel walking into her office was a little different.

He looked good, but he usually did. Like a polished financial advisor with a compelling smile and an easy air, chestnut hair, well-dressed and confident, except his usual charm was not as easy and on the surface.

"You wanted to talk to me?"

She equivocated. "On the phone."

"That's friendly." His tone was sarcastic.

"I'm not trying to be friendly. I just have a question or two." That did not include a visit to her office.

"Okay, go ahead. You are good at those."

"I'm a district attorney. I should hope so."

He took a seat by her desk without invitation. "I'm aware. So?"

"Daniel, someone is harassing me and I want to know if you have any clue to who it might be? A dark-haired woman."

"That's why you wanted to talk?"

She looked him in the eye. "I don't know who she is or what she wants. Please tell me if you think *you* might know something. You started contacting me, and then she started following me."

"Dammit, Stephanie, I thought you wanted to maybe talk to *me*."

"About what?"

"Us."

"There is no us."

"There could be again."

He was dreaming if he thought that was true.

Since he was sitting right there she took out her phone and pushed a couple of buttons to pull up the picture. "Who is she?"

To his credit, he did look at the screen. "I have no idea."

"Never seen her before?"

"I just said that."

"No, you didn't, you said you didn't know who she was, not the same thing. I just wanted clarification. You've never seen her before?"

He gave her a level look and his signature engaging smile. "I'm taking a trip down memory lane and remembering what conversations with you were like."

His problem was she knew that charm was superficial, always just designed to get him what he wanted.

If what he wanted was her, he could forget it.

"It was nice of you to take the time to stop by. I wish you'd have solved the problem, but I'll have to look at it from

154

another angle. So she isn't an ex-girlfriend or anyone that resents you calling me?"

"No. Have dinner with me?"

That didn't come out of the blue exactly since he'd been calling her, but she was entirely uninterested.

"I'm sorry, I'm seeing someone."

That smile vanished. "Who? Let me guess. Austin?"

How would he guess that? Back to suspect number one. "Why do you think I'd be seeing Trey?"

"Oh, let's see, we break it off and he gets immediately divorced. Go figure. He's always been interested in you."

"Daniel, Anna filed for divorce. It had nothing to do with me. That was between the two of them."

"Right." His expression was tight when he stood, and if he thought she wasn't friendly, his stance was a clear indication of his angst. "I guess I'm not surprised."

"I never said it was him."

"You don't have to say it."

No goodbye, he just left, but she hadn't wanted to see him anyway so if he was offended she'd moved on, that was really his problem, whether it was Trey or not.

She was still off balance from the fact someone had targeted both her and Trey, and wished if she'd had to have the face to face, it could have produced better results in the form of an actual answer.

It was hard to say if Daniel was culpable but she'd liked to think that she could see through him after some experience with his deceptive personality, so maybe he was not responsible. It still left them in the dark, but maybe elimination would work.

She texted Trey. *So much for no personal interaction because Daniel came by my office, and from his reaction he didn't recognize the woman who put the device on my car. He can convince with the best of them, but I know him. I don't think he was lying.*

It was telling that she was nervous until he finally called back an hour later. "Sorry, I had a meeting. What? He just showed up?"

155

"Large as life. I really have not had a perfect day."

"What can I do to make it better?"

Ask that question was the answer. "If I knew I'd tell you."

"And if you told me I'd do it."

"Hold me close tonight."

"Steph, that's a given."

"I'm in love with you."

Why the hell did she say that? She just hung up and sat there wondering what the hell she was doing with her life . . . except she was fairly sure she just blurted out something completely true and never waited for a response.

What was she doing to him too?

Luckily, it was Trey and he could deal with it, or she certainly had confidence he could.

The divorce had nothing to do with her.

Did it?

CHAPTER NINETEEN

They were together.

There was just no question about it. Such an interesting dynamic.

If I could only be the proverbial fly on the wall and hear their conversation.

Luckily, I have an inventive imagination.

Why am I so interested?

Because they could have a profound effect on my life.

* * *

It snowed in Tennessee in October.

In a sense it was on the romantic side, soft white flakes coming down outside the windows, and he'd opened a nice bottle of Merlot to go with the Italian food Stephanie had made for dinner, so one would think it was a nice evening.

But there was no doubt she was unusually quiet, and Trey had a feeling it wasn't so much the events of the day as what she'd said to him on the phone.

I'm in love with you.

So if she didn't want to talk about it, he could let it go until she did.

It certainly had improved his day.

He knew how he felt about her and why he had agreed to her unusual request and if they would share a child, it would be better if reciprocal feelings were involved.

"The tortellini is delicious," he said. "So tell me, what did Hanover have to say?"

She seemed relieved he wasn't going to bring up her remark, which he suspected had been impulsive and maybe a direct result of Daniel's unexpected visit, yet hopefully sincere. "I pointed out we were both professionals and would handle ourselves that way, and he seemed to accept that. Like I said on the phone, if he wasn't co-counsel, I bet he'd remove me."

"Since I doubt we'll go to trial, it hardly matters."

"True enough. I know plenty of lawyers married to other lawyers and they sleep together obviously, so it isn't an ethical question other than we are opposing counsel. I'm sure his concern is that this case will be high profile if we end up in court and if someone is out to sabotage either the defense or the prosecution, our relationship could become fodder for the media."

He took a sip of wine and put his elbows inelegantly on the table. "I think that's what has me stymied. If it isn't Daniel, and you said after talking to him you don't think it is, it has to be tied to one of us, or the case. Richard Dorset asked me if Anna might be the culprit, but no. I'm sure you agree with that."

Stephanie shook her head. "She would never do something so underhanded. In fact, I expect we would have a conversation neither one of us would enjoy if she knew, so she doesn't know. She's upfront and sometimes too honest with her opinions."

"Tell me about it."

"But she is also one of the best people I know."

"I don't disagree. If you remember, and I know you do because you were there, I married her."

Stephanie propped her chin on her fist and gazed at him, her eyes glimmering in the muted light of his dining room. "Did you divorce her because of me? Daniel seemed to think so."

"No, *she* divorced *me* because of you."

That was about as honest as he could be.

Her lips parted but she said nothing for a few moments. Then she sighed. "I would never have asked that if I hadn't had a second glass of wine. So if my powers of comprehension are working properly, she constantly accused you of cheating on her, and she thought it was with me? Did I just draw the right conclusion?"

"That's pretty accurate."

"How could she ever think I'd do that to her?" Stephanie looked outraged and hurt.

"How could she ever think I would do it to her either?" he countered. "And you, of all people, know it to be true that I did not."

They just looked at each other for a long telling moment.

"I thought she wasn't talking to me because she was just upset about the marriage not working out. But now—"

He interrupted her. "No, stop right there. We aren't betraying her in any way. She and I are not together and haven't been for quite some time. I have absolutely no issues with her personal life because it is no longer my business. She's free to do as she pleases and I wish her all the best. I should get the same consideration, and like I just pointed out, we did nothing wrong."

"I think the problem is she's not over you."

He had no comment on that. Anna had not shared her feelings with him for a long time. "I hope this doesn't impact your friendship, but I suppose it has already."

"For all we know she got one of those not-so-nice communications as well."

"Oh, I think we would have heard something by now, so I doubt that." He wasn't sure how to ask the question, but since their private relationship was hardly a secret any longer, maybe they should discuss it. "If you should get pregnant, what are you going to tell everyone? I have to admit I've been wondering."

"I was going to ask you what you wanted me to say, but I hardly think it is a state secret now that you and I are involved."

159

He fingered the stem of his glass and muttered, "I hope my grandmother didn't get that notice, but otherwise, like I said, I don't see why anyone should care about two consenting adults spending time together in bed or otherwise."

"Anna might."

"If she does we'll know about it and just deal with it. Once again, she can do whatever she wants and I would never say a word one way or the other."

"Can I ask you a question?"

"Of course you can, but can you make it an easy one, please? I had a day I think similar to the one you had." He decided to refill his glass from the half empty bottle.

There was no real accumulation outside, just a gentle dusting of white, but enough to notice. Out the window the lawn glistened and reflected the moonlight.

Stephanie spoke and it was quiet. "Did you and Anna talk about having children?"

"Some, but we decided to wait. I think deep down we both knew we just weren't meant for each other as a poet might put it. Or perhaps a psychologist could define it better, I don't know. I'm neither one. Unfortunately a lot of people make the same mistake we did."

"I didn't talk about it with Daniel. I should have. That was my error right there. I assumed he wanted what I wanted, but I made myriad mistakes with him. I honestly never wanted to see him again and at least you don't feel like that about Anna."

That was accurate only to a point. "Well, we can still be civil with each other usually once she speaks her mind. The storm needs to pass and then she's over it."

"We really have been friends for so long I hope she and I can weather this."

"Weather me being in the picture?" He said it ironically. "I think that's been an issue since the day I met you. Instant attraction — I tried to ignore it but wasn't able to conceal it very well evidently since Anna and Daniel figured it out with no problem."

Not to mention Richard, and he suspected a few other colleagues as well that saw he and Stephanie interact fairly often. Maybe he should have skipped law school for acting classes.

"I'm transparent as well, I guess, if Anna thought you might be cheating on her with me."

"We aren't cheating on anyone. Anna and I would have gone our separate ways even without you in the picture, and I get the impression of the same with you and Daniel."

"The latter is certainly true." Stephanie smoothed back her hair behind her left ear in that mannerism he knew well. She did it in court too when she was really thinking something over. "I question my judgment every single time when I think of him. Maybe I'm not as smart as I think I am."

"You are one of the most intelligent people I know, but when it comes to relationships, I think logic doesn't really apply in a reliable fashion."

"Maybe not. I'm still processing what I said to you."

* * *

If nothing else she was learning the difference between sex, and passionate lovemaking.

Stephanie had the college boyfriend who had coaxed her into going to bed with him, and of course she'd met Daniel, and he had a true talent for convincing people to do anything he wanted. But Trey was an intense and focused lover, and as she lay in the breathless aftermath, she thought he was very good at it.

The ringing phone ruined the moment of post-coital intimacy, and it was getting pretty late.

It wasn't hers, it was Trey's. He muttered a low curse, rolled to the side of the bed and snatched it up. "Who the hell would call me now? It's late."

"At least it wasn't a few moments ago." She was still languid in the aftermath.

"I'm going to take that attitude too. Oh hell, it's Detective Bailey. My apologies, I'm going to take this one."

She agreed, levering up on one elbow. "Absolutely, answer it."

The gist of the conversation was pretty clear to her from just hearing one side of it and Trey's terse replies, and as a prosecutor naked in bed with a defense attorney, she knew that most people would just laugh at the situation.

She wasn't laughing. When Trey ended the call, she said, "So let me get this straight, Colin got out of his ankle bracelet somehow and escaped? That's not going to help him in court."

"Don't I know it. Bailey came home to an empty house."

"He's helping me win the case I don't want to win in the first place."

Trey settled back down next to her. "I know. Bailey can't believe it either. Now he's lost the kid charged with three murders."

"Colin is smart. Why would he do this?"

"I don't want to call his father and tell him he skipped bail."

She was startled. "His father? That's how he made bail?"

He pulled her close, his dark hair rumpled probably thanks to her fingers running through it, and said evenly, "Steph, I know you are naked in my arms right now, and I would probably give you anything you asked me for, but I'm not telling you that. I just said too much. Let's hope Bailey can find Colin and leave it there."

His mouth found a very sensitive spot just between her ear and her jaw. It really was distracting, she had to admit it.

In a very pleasurable way.

"I bet he went to that cabin of Bailey's. And met his girlfriend there."

"You think so?" Trey lifted his head and looked at her. "I suppose that does make sense. He's got his phone back, so of course he's called her. I'm leaving that part of all this in Bailey's capable hands. He volunteered for the job, after all."

"For one thing, he doesn't lock that place so Colin knows he can walk right back in."

"I trust your instincts. Surely Bailey will think of that. How Colin got out of that bracelet escapes me. My understanding is that those are pretty secure."

"My understanding is Alcatraz was supposed to be unescapable."

"He is a smart kid. No one can deny that."

"Should we offer to help Bailey find him?"

His dark brows went up. "This time of night together? That's another memo right there."

"Since the whole rest of the world seems to know we've spent the night doing what we just did, I'm sure Bailey has figured it out. I know Colin caught on we had more than just a professional acquaintance when we arrived the other evening."

"I'll call Bailey back and ask if he wants our help, how's that?"

"It's your client on the run."

"Yes, it is." His voice did not reflect much happiness. "And here I thought my day had improved so much."

"He just wanted to see her, I'm sure. Realistically, he can't go far without money or family. Let's face it, he's young and really in over his head."

"Everyone knows that, even him, and yet he does this."

"Because he's seventeen."

"Are we sure we want to have children?" His mouth quirked as he picked up his phone. "I'll call. I certainly want to do something about the situation if I can, though I'd rather just stay in bed with you."

That question had included a plural she didn't necessarily expect, but then again she'd started this.

Or maybe it had started long before she realized it had, it was hard to say.

"You already know my answer is yes to children and I would like to help Colin."

"Let's see if Bailey wants our help or not."

CHAPTER TWENTY

Going off the grid held a certain appeal. It might even be a good idea.
I wasn't sure.
But I couldn't allow it.
There were some lines in the sand, drawn there for a purpose.

* * *

This was not the finest evening ever and he'd had some bad ones.

Homicides, accidents, and the worst were maybe domestic violence calls when he was just a deputy and none of it was pleasant.

Chris was a police officer and a teenager had escaped his supervision and had done it so easily he was surprised and not happy in the least.

On the other hand, if he could just catch up with Colin, it might break this case.

That was the key.

Lucky for him, the fugitive texted.

Sorry.

That was fine. Now he had a location.

Ms. St. James was right. On the phone Austin said she thought that as it was secluded and private Colin might head to his river cabin.

He listened.

It wasn't like Colin had many choices and that small compact car parked in the drive was not his, so Colin had either stolen it or had company. Chris doubted boosting cars was something he was skilled at, so someone had picked him up. When he pulled in he actually debated what to do.

He called Anna. "Okay, I found him. Or else some drifter is in my cabin that has a car. I'm debating how to announce my arrival but not interrupt an intimate moment. I'm good with some stuff, but probably not teen sex. That might be more you, Ms. Psychologist. Thoughts on how I should handle this?"

"You didn't have teen sex?"

He gave a muffled laugh. "Oh, no comment there."

"Just knock loudly before you walk in."

"I knew you were the one to ask. They are young and we are past the tipping point since she's already pregnant. He's in deep trouble so I figure that's what they might be doing, and they really could use time together. I just wish he'd asked me."

"Do you want me to come and be there when you talk with him?"

"Actually I think Austin is on his way. He is Colin's attorney so I called him first because I don't want any issues there. I just wanted to let you know what is going on." He looked at the bundle of fur on the seat next to him. "Besides, I have backup in the form of the moppet."

He was also convinced the girlfriend, Emily, was the one that had called him, but she'd borrowed the phone of a friend. That much he'd figured out when he traced down the number but there was zero cooperation. The answer to his question to her parents was their daughter had no idea who might use her phone.

Loyalty was apparently not dead.

If Emily had information, he really wanted to hear it. Having an attorney and a district attorney present would be helpful because he knew they'd arrive together again.

If either of St. James or Austin thought the relationship was a secret, they were mistaken, but on his part he had the confession of the night he'd picked up the at least slightly inebriated Ms. St. James to educate him on why she'd had more to drink more than she should have.

At least for them, it seemed to have worked out.

The question was would Anna Hernandez agree with that assessment of the situation?

"Well, I'd appreciate a call when it is all under control again."

"Will do."

He got out of the car and walked to the door but it opened before he could knock. Colin stood there, a little rumpled and there was no surprise — or apology — in his expression. "I knew you'd figure it out but we really needed to see each other. Hope you don't mind we used your place. Our choices are kind of limited."

"I'd like to think I'm a reasonable man. You could have just asked me if this would be okay."

Colin avoided looking him in the eyes by bending to pet the dog, who was delighted to see him of course, and leaping up and down. "Yeah well, you might have said no. I couldn't take the chance."

"How'd you ever dismantle the ankle bracelet?"

"I'm wearing it. I just disarmed it. I'm pretty good at stuff like that, and hey, I sent you an apology."

"So you did. Mind if I come in?"

"Oh, sorry . . . It's your cabin." He stepped back. "Uh, this is Emily. Em, this is Detective Bailey."

She was sitting on the couch and had the same vaguely disheveled look, like she'd pulled on her jeans and sweatshirt quickly and was obviously a little embarrassed. "Hi."

Young. Hopefully not too young. That was hardly another charge Colin needed. Pretty girl, dark hair, light-brown eyes,

166

smooth skin and a shapely build that didn't show the pregnancy but then again, she was wearing loose clothes. Chris said neutrally, "Hi and it is nice to meet you. I think maybe you left me a message, didn't you?"

She looked uncertainly at Colin and he shrugged. "If you did, you did."

"I was trying to help you," she said to him.

"I know."

Chris guessed she was sixteen or so, not that Colin was of legal age either, but considering he was being tried as an adult already on felony charges he hardly needed that. Eighteen was the legal age of consent, but she clearly wasn't that. However, he wasn't four years older, so he should be in the clear. Neither of them was able to consent according to the statue of the state of Tennessee for statutory rape.

It just muddied the waters and Chris could live without it, but there was a clear stream somewhere. If counsel couldn't bring a charge, they could still bring it to the attention of the court he had a younger pregnant girlfriend as a stain against his character. Juries listened even if it wasn't able to be admitted, but that was Austin's problem, not his.

"What did you want to tell me?" He casually walked to the refrigerator and took out a bottle of water, doing his best to not betray he was intensely interested in what Emily had to say. No question he'd rather have a beer, but it was late and he'd have to drive home. This wasn't his only case to handle and he had a full schedule pretty much all the time. This cabin was for a rare day or two off. "Your message was you could prove Colin wasn't guilty."

"I know someone who has killed two people before. They did it."

To say it caught his attention was an understatement. "Okay, but you do realize I am required to investigate any sort of serious accusation of that kind." The case really needed a pivotal moment. "Go on."

"I can tell you the exact night it happened."

He had an eyewitness to a murder? "Can you tell me who the victims are?"

"She killed my grandparents." Her eyes filled with tears and she swiped at her cheek as one escaped. "They were so nice. I'm sorry. I've been crying a lot lately."

He needed names, but she was young, pregnant, and distraught so he didn't press for details, he just waited. If she wanted to say more, he was extremely interested, but then again, he wasn't going to push a young girl in her situation especially after what she'd just said.

Colin went to sit next to her and in a touching gesture held her hand. "It's okay."

The good news was Chris heard a vehicle pull up. That was one nice thing about the cabin. It was dead silent outside other than the gentle rush of the river and an occasional night bird once evening set in, so no one could really surprise you unless they crept up on foot. He couldn't imagine why they'd want to and that was why he didn't bother to lock the place up.

He could use Stephanie St. James and he wanted Austin right there so he could see that while his client had violated his ankle restraint, he hadn't skipped bail.

"We have company and I'd really like to continue this conversation with more adults present, because what I never want to happen is to have evidence or testimony thrown out because it is my word against yours. You have rights and I respect them. There's a reason police officers question suspects or witnesses with more people present and you both are still considered juveniles. This way, everyone is protected and we can make sure the interview is not questioned."

"Trey and Ms. St. James?"

"You guessed it. I also need them both to know you didn't really jump bail."

Colin looked fine with it and told Emily, "It's cool."

"Okay." She nodded, still sniffling.

Nothing about the situation was okay really except he didn't lose his charge and he was really wondering now if her

168

grandparents had the last name McConnell. Those victims had been an older couple.

That might explain a lot.

* * *

It wasn't that Trey didn't take Bailey's word, but walking into the cabin and seeing Colin sitting there on the well-worn couch was a relief.

At least he didn't have to call Senator Grayson and inform him he'd forfeited quite a not-so-small fortune on behalf of the son he'd just recently met.

Now he just needed to find out what was going on. So he sat down, took a moment, and just asked reasonably, "It's late, we're all tired . . . is there something specific that precipitated dodging out of a contained situation in which you were secure and not in confinement to risk going back into custody again? Talk to me."

Colin set his jaw and looked back defiantly. "I needed to talk to Emily."

"I believe Detective Bailey gave you back your phone. You could talk to her."

"She can't stay at home."

Trey looked at Bailey, who also looked perplexed.

"I can't." The girl sitting next to Colin clutching his hand agreed. "And Colin needs to stay with Detective Bailey but we talked about it and neither one of us is safe. He's out on bail, and that isn't perfect."

"What's the threat?" Stephanie did what she did best and honed in. "Let's be clear. Saying vaguely you are in danger does not help us define the situation."

Firm, but said with purpose.

"My mother."

The girl started to cry and if there had been a toss-up between whether he or Bailey were more uncomfortable, it would have been a tie, but it did not faze Stephanie.

"You're afraid of her. That's not a question, that's statement of fact." Steph took a moment, and this was why she

169

was such a good attorney, she always weighed her words. "She's unhappy you're pregnant."

Emily nodded.

"So you think she might harm you, or Colin."

"Him, for sure."

"I deal with clear facts. He is responsible, correct?"

With surprising composure through her tears, Emily said, "We both are."

Stephanie agreed and Trey could sense she resisted an urge to look at him. "Well, yes, it does take two. What makes you so convinced she might be dangerous?"

"I don't know what to do. I have nowhere to go."

"You did not answer my question, but as far as somewhere to go, that can be arranged. A safe place will be found for you. It seems to me that away from her might be best in your opinion since you are here by choice."

It was Bailey that said calmly, "Tell me about your grandparents."

"Em, you told me, so tell them. If what we both think happened is true, he can help." Colin urged her by touching her damp cheek. "Think of your dad."

"I don't want to."

"Me either."

"It's our fault."

"I know."

It seemed to Trey that all three of the adults in the room had a lightning flash of insight at that moment because Stephanie gave him a startled look and Bailey's expression changed as well.

Oh hell.

It was his turn. Trey said in a tone he had to carefully control, "Are you Joe Gaines's *daughter*?"

She nodded, more tears welling. "My parents fought all the time, she constantly took him to court to contest any custody. It was awful. I don't remember when it wasn't terrible. Sometimes I got to see my dad but a lot of times, she just wouldn't let me."

170

Colin pointed out defensively, "We aren't blood related in any way."

But if Joe had partial custody, they'd known each other for a long time, probably played together as children, grown into adolescence aware of each other, it wasn't quite that much of a surprise.

No wonder Colin had kept their relationship a secret. Dating your stepsister wasn't incest, but hardy ideal. Getting her pregnant was bound to make everyone unhappy.

As a defense attorney he was already recalculating. If Joe Gaines had been angry with him — and what father wouldn't be no matter how close their relationship — it gave Colin a solid motive to kill his stepfather. On the other hand, if Emily's mother was angry about it and felt it happened on her ex-husband's watch, then she had a very solid motive indeed.

If she really was unstable and dangerous.

"I don't think the blame falls on either of you. Tell us about your grandparents." Trey could persuade a jury, so surely he could influence a young girl to at least talk to them and Colin was clearly on his side. "This situation needs to be resolved and I think every person in this room agrees that Colin is not responsible for those three deaths that he's been charged with, and apparently one of the victims is your father. I'm here to make sure Colin doesn't pay for crimes he didn't commit and he has a future. Please talk to Detective Bailey."

Stephanie backed him up. "It would be so helpful."

Emily took a moment, but said haltingly, "I just don't really know anything. Okay, this is it. One night my mom came home and there was a lot of blood on her and she immediately washed her clothes. Then I heard three days later my grandparents were dead, but not from her. She didn't tell me anything. Both at the same time? I was only thirteen, but I . . . wondered. And now my dad? When I heard he was dead, I just had this terrible feeling."

That was both informative and helpful.

He looked at Bailey. "You have those prints."

"I do."

"Those will make or break this case."

Bailey argued that assumption. "Maybe, maybe not. I can bring her in for questioning and see if her prints match, but I don't know if it will help Colin at this point. He's been arrested and charged and you're a defense attorney, it can be argued that somehow he took the gun from her or Emily gave it to him. As for the murders of her parents, she can claim she was in their kitchen and used the knife to help her mother cook by chopping up vegetables or something like that, and it was just handy for whoever killed them. Circumstantial at this point and she'll know she's under suspicion and I'll only have the memory of a thirteen-year-old girl that she washed her clothes on an evening close to the murders."

"He's right." Stephanie said it with conviction. "Without the direct connection it goes straight back to the fact I could win in court, admit it, Trey."

"Yes, it complicates things." Under his breath he muttered an expletive.

Bailey stated grimly, "But the timing is right. Emily, tell me, does anyone else in your family think your mother might be responsible for the death of your grandparents?"

She answered readily. "My Uncle Jack. He came to our house and accused her and that's how I found out they were dead."

"I'd like to talk to him."

"I can give you his name and where he works. She won't let me speak to him or my aunt and I would ask them for help, but look at what happened to my dad."

That was certainly a valid point.

"I'll find him," said Bailey with conviction.

CHAPTER TWENTY-ONE

The irrational thing was my outrage was surreal to me, so I was making mistakes, directing my anger at the people who could truly do me harm, as if I didn't care any longer, and maybe I didn't.

When my parents died I expected the worst, but it didn't happen.

So I'm apparently operating under that expectation now. I don't know.

* * *

Being called into the office was never a fun experience.

Sheriff Lawrence was unhappy and he wasn't a man to conceal his current state of mind. He lifted his bushy brows. "Can I get this straight, son, you knew the girl was a runaway and didn't report it. Then let her stay overnight in the company of a young man charged with felony murder. That's correct?"

Chris simply responded, "Yes." That was the truth and he didn't deny it. "It was late and I was with them by the way. It wasn't like they were alone."

He left out the part that they had been alone before he caught up with them, but it seemed to him they were both pretty in need of each other and it wouldn't alter this conversation.

"Her mother complained to this department and who knows else when her daughter showed up at school this morning after being gone all night and you were the one who dropped her off."

"I don't think that woman should complain too loudly."

There was one thing about Lawrence, he was a good old boy, but he was also sharp as a newly polished axe blade. "Explain."

"I believe it is possible she's killed five people and, you know what, I have a defense lawyer and a certain district attorney that are of the same mind."

"Okay, now you have my attention." Lawrence leaned back in his chair and rubbed his jaw.

"I'll have your attention when I have her prints. Until then, I've got nothing but a seventeen-year-old boy charged with murder because he insisted we do it to protect his pregnant girlfriend."

"Oh Jesus, what a mess. Five victims? I thought you were looking into a triple homicide."

"Remember the unsolved double murder of the older couple on the farm in the southern part of the county three years ago? Maybe we can lay that one to rest."

"The stabbings?"

"That's the one."

Lawrence frowned. "It has always bothered me. I knew the McConnells. Not well, but they went to the same church as some friends of ours who always ask about the investigation. Are you serious?"

"I am."

"Then get on it. Why are we sitting here? Where's Carter?"

Lawrence had been the one to call him into his office, but Chris didn't mention that because he was glad to get the meeting over since he'd gotten a prompt reply from Emily's uncle that he'd be glad to have a conversation. "He's coming with me to an interview. People tend to take him more seriously."

"He looks like a detective, not a backwoods youngster with boots and a badge." Lawrence said it with a hint of humor.

Chris didn't take offense. "I know. The day you told me I could ditch the uniform was one of the happiest of my life."

"Glad I could make your day, now go make mine and let me know how all this goes."

"Will do."

Carter was at his desk, looking at his computer screen but he pressed the log out button when Chris walked up. "We all set to go?"

"Yeah. He said three o'clock." He looked at his partner, who did look nicely professional in a shirt and tie and tailored slacks. "Explain to me why a woman who I am sure wonders if she's under a microscope right now, would call the sheriff's department to complain about my conduct as a police officer and draw attention to the whole thing?"

"You're the one who wants to be a profiler. You tell me."

"She's wacko."

Carter stood and just looked at him. "Technical term? Good choice. I think all people who murder other people are in that category by the way. Let's go talk to her brother and ask him if he agrees so we can maybe get some tangible evidence."

"It was just pointed out to me that I don't have the same conservative presence you do, so I'm aware it might be better if you asked the questions."

"You do shoot from the hip more often than me."

"Good, you get to drive. He works in Knoxville and I'm going to sleep in the car. Last night was a late one."

"How lucky am I? Could you at least clue me in on what happened?"

"Somehow that kid was able to deactivate his ankle bracelet and he went AWOL. I have no idea how he accomplished that. Girlfriend picked him up and they went to my cabin, which was a pretty good choice, you have to admit, since no one would find them. I did catch up with them when I came home and realized he was gone. I talked to Austin, and he and Stephanie St. James arrived not long after me, so I was able to question both minors with counsel present. Emily was the one who told me she thought maybe her mother was responsible for the death of her grandparents, so it will be easy enough to connect the dots because of the fingerprints."

"If they are hers."

"Exactly. If they aren't, we are back at square one. According to Emily, her uncle labels her mother as his main suspect and has directly accused her."

"Did she say why he thought that?"

They walked out of the office toward the car. "No. It seems to me to be murder of impulse. I have no clue as to why the woman might kill her own parents, but it is hardly without precedent. Those murders are an unsolved case. It fits the second scenario when she might have gone looking for Colin Simon, he wasn't home, and instead she just killed everyone there. In any case, according to her daughter, she hated her ex-husband."

"You're serious about this?"

"Yes, I am. There's no premeditation. That's why I don't want to just bring her in for questioning, we need enough to arrest. I'm convinced she went into that house looking for Colin. I don't want to just ignite a fire I can't contain. There's a reason he wanted to be charged and I know it is because he fears Emily is in danger if her mother feels cornered."

Carter opened the driver's door. "Then let's go find out if her brother can help us with that endeavor."

Chris did at least close his eyes and doze off for a while during the journey because he hadn't exaggerated, he'd been up most of the night, but it wasn't like insomnia and he were strangers. He was also aware that there was someone not quite rational out there and he wanted to be awake if they came knocking at his door. He most certainly had his sidearm handy, but then again, he always did because it was part of the job.

Jeff McConnell worked in management for a retail distribution center and the place was busy, but they were directed easily enough to his office. He proved to be mid-thirties or so, dark-haired, his demeanor pleasant enough, but when he shook hands and offered them chairs in front of his desk, his expression did darken. "So you want to talk to me about my parents' deaths. I can't think of another reason a homicide detective would call me and ask for a few minutes of my time."

Carter was master of an understated point that got through. "That's not a closed case and we're not going to let it slide. I'm sure you agree."

McConnell said with grim emphasis, "Oh, I do."

"Tell us about your sister."

"Jennifer?"

"We have information you thought, at least at one time, she might have been involved."

He sat back and closed his eyes briefly. "I hate it, but I still do."

"Can you tell us why?"

There was a hesitation, but he explained slowly, "She's just never been quite right. I know that's vague, but I grew up with her childhood tantrums and you just never could see them coming, you know? My mother took them in her stride and excused them, cleaned up the broken glasses or the heirloom vase slammed into the wall, but it was clear to me that there was a serious lack of control there with the right trigger. Most of the time she's fine, but she can snap. I've seen it. I have absolutely no evidence she did anything, but if you want the truth, when I got the news my parents had been violently killed in their sleep, it was the first thing that came to my mind."

"We understand you confronted her about it. What did she say?" Carter was his usual self, calm and reserved.

"Nothing. Please understand, I was in absolute shock, and maybe so was she, but possibly not for the same reason, I don't know. No denial, but no admission. She just looked at me."

177

Chris had to ask a question. "Do you worry about your niece?"

The answer was swift and succinct. "I worry about Emily's safety every day. Let me put it in clear terms. When we were little, I think I was about six so Jen was ten, she wanted a kitten. Begged for it. My parents got one for her birthday. Everything was fine, but one day it scratched Jennifer. And then I never saw it again. I asked my mother and she said it must have gotten out and run away, but she was crying when she said it. I know Jen killed it."

"Any reason she might have to harm your parents?"

"She was constantly borrowing money and they weren't all that well off in the first place. I finally told them to just tell her no. She continually changed jobs and I doubt it was because she quit, it was probably a tendency to get fired. I thought maybe it would force her to calm down a little if she was made to support herself and Emily just on her own." He exhaled audibly. "I can tell you that I've wondered if that advice got them killed."

When they walked out, Carter was silent until they were in the car and headed back south. "That was disturbing as hell."

"We need her prints." Chris agreed. He could have lived his whole life without the implications of the kitten story, but the truth was, it could have run away. However, two people did not stab themselves to death, and neither did three people shoot themselves in bed.

"Yes, we do."

"I guess I technically have Emily's car. I made them both ride to my house with me so they wouldn't have an escape vehicle and that is why I drove her to school. She said she could take the bus home."

"Surely her mother has been in that vehicle. See if one good crime tech could lift a print?"

"I think it is worth a try, but we have a bigger problem. How can we even possibly let Emily go home? Obviously her mother knows the sheriff's department is involved and I do not want that young vulnerable girl in the care of someone unstable who might be feeling like she has nothing to lose."

"Call Ms. Hernandez and ask about options."

Chris picked up his phone. "I have thought of that already."

* * *

Anna waited outside the principal's office in a chair. The students streamed out, but one of them was escorted by a teacher. She was a dark-haired girl with delicate features and wore a baggy sweatshirt and an anxious expression.

She sincerely wished she could say she hadn't seen that expression before, but she certainly had far too many times. It was the unasked question: *what's wrong now.*

"Emily Gaines?" She stood and smiled. "I'm Ms. Hernandez. Detective Bailey sent me to pick you up. I hope it is okay if you skip the bus and I take you back to his house so we can have a conversation."

"Is Colin okay?"

"Actually, I'm his social worker, and Colin is fine, doing his classwork from remote as we speak. Please feel free to ask the principal if it is okay to go with me. I'll wait here. I've signed in and they have my name and know I came to get you."

The girl looked relieved. "That's alright. I hate the bus anyway. If you know Colin and Detective Bailey, I'm fine."

"Let's go then."

They walked out together and Anna motioned to her car. "I get to park close. You aren't the first child to exit this building with social services."

"I'm not a child. I haven't been one for a long time."

Anna could have argued that on terms of age, but she didn't. She understood the sentiment, even if she still thought Emily was rather young. Some of the children she dealt with had been through a lot in their lives no matter their age. "We'll go and talk about what happens next."

179

"Why would that change anything?"

"I understand you don't know me, but we can discuss it. Person to person. With Colin and Detective Bailey there if you want."

"My mother?"

"Her, yes, if you want her present but if you don't, that's fine too."

"I don't."

That spoke volumes.

Anna unlocked the car with a push of a button on her key fob. "My job is to make sure you are as safe and protected as possible. If you don't want her part of the equation, then I listen to *your* voice. I am an advocate, not a police officer."

"Thanks."

"Emily, this is what I do. If you think I'm not there for Colin, think again. He has no one else now but Detective Bailey, me and you."

"I know."

Well, perhaps his father. In Chris's brief call — and he was a man of few words — he simply asked if she could pick up Emily Gaines from high school, it was related to the murder case, and he'd meet her at his house.

He also had asked if she'd like to have dinner with him.

Well, them. Colin would be there as well, and she thought now Emily as well. That was fine, she needed to know what exactly was going on. So that was a definitive yes.

Emily dropped her backpack on to the floor of the car and climbed in the passenger side. Her eyes were wide and troubled. "What does my mother know?"

"The truth. That you've been taken by social services because she reported you as a runaway, and that we would be in touch once we assessed the situation after talking to you."

"She's going to be really mad."

"What happens when she gets really mad?"

"Nothing good." The curtain of her dark hair concealed her expression as she bent her head.

"Keeping in mind I talk to children of abusive parents all too often, is she physical with you?"

"Sometimes."

"How often?"

The question was evaded. "I just needed to see Colin."

"Are you afraid of her?"

The girl looked at her and said with frightening sincerity, "I'd be stupid if I wasn't."

CHAPTER TWENTY-TWO

It was as if I was a runaway train now.

All I wanted was to go off those tracks or miss a switch and derail into a crowded station.

There was a certain freedom in it.

* * *

The situation was escalating, both on a professional and personal level.

Someone had left an envelope on her car, neatly tucked under the left wiper blade. Stephanie just stood there and looked at it with apprehension as soon as she caught sight of it. After a moment she told herself it could be anything, an advertisement — that was illegal but not all people knew that or some just didn't care, but still . . .

Carefully — it was rare but occasionally prints could be lifted from paper — she took it by one corner and gingerly lifted it and opened it. It wasn't sealed.

There were two pictures and a slip of paper.

She stood there very still, and felt a chill course through her body. The first picture was from fairly far away, but she clearly remembered the moment of that kiss when she'd arrived at Trey's house a few days ago and he'd greeted her with such impetuous enthusiasm in the doorway.

The second one was of a dark window reflecting the moonlight.

The note said: *I know where you both sleep.*

With hands that shook she pulled out her phone and called Trey. To her relief, he answered and she couldn't even speak for a moment until she managed to say, "Where are you?"

"Just getting ready to leave my office . . . everything okay?"

"I . . . well, I'm not sure."

"Steph?"

"I think we both just got obliquely threatened, or maybe it isn't that vague, you can tell me when I show it to you."

"Show me what?"

"What are we doing tonight anyway?"

"I assumed having a nice evening together. You sound fairly shaken and you don't shake easily."

"I believe you might also find it disturbing. Something is happening to escalate this case and I'm forming a theory, but let me process. I'll stop at the grocery store on my way and we can stay in and discuss this. I'll cook, it's fine. I consider it therapy with food at the end of the session. Your house has a better security system."

"Of course I'll agree to that but why does my security system figure in?"

"Tell me you like pork chops."

"Yes, I do, but what the hell are we talking about?"

"I'll see you soon."

She couldn't be sure the source of that disturbing message wasn't watching, so she unlocked her car and slid in and pulled away as quickly as possible. It wasn't like she didn't know someone was out there.

But why?

It could still be related to Daniel, but she doubted it now more than ever.

She did stop and shop, surreptitiously looking over her shoulder and didn't see anyone following, but then again she had a picture indicating they knew exactly where she was going to make dinner and spend the night, so why follow.

There was no doubt this was challenging in more ways than one.

Obviously both she and Trey assumed they'd be together that night and, even though it should be a private thing, so did a murderer.

Nice.

The slide into their relationship felt natural, like they'd maybe both just been waiting for it. There had always been an awareness of each other between them, and apparently other people had noticed because Daniel usually was not insightful. She'd learned that the hard way.

She really needed to talk to Anna about it somehow, she just wasn't sure how to do it, and had more pressing issues on her table at the moment.

The stop at home was swift, just a change of clothes and she was out of there.

It was a relief to see Trey open the door immediately as she pulled in, safe and sound, coming out to help her with the grocery bags, his eyes full of concern. "What's going on?"

"Let's go inside, give me a glass of wine, and I'll explain."

"Sounds like a plan, I guess, since I'm in the dark."

"You won't be in a minute."

He carried everything in, she followed and he provided the wine and poured a glass for himself as well. She waited until they both sat down at the kitchen counter before she handed over the envelope. "What do you make of this?"

He looked at the pictures first, then read the slip of paper, and looked at the pictures again. When he glanced up at her, his face was set. "It seems to me to be a clear message."

"Is the threat against me or you?"

"I can't tell. It was left on your car, but surely anyone that would send pictures to both our offices indicating we are sexually involved would know you would share it with me,

184

so that means nothing. They would expect you'd give me the information. It could be either one of us."

She felt better he had the same reaction she did. "Either this is tied to Daniel, or it is the case and I am thinking the latter. 'I know where you both sleep' and the victims have all been killed in their beds while sleeping?"

"I agree."

"How do they get into the houses without forced entry? It really could be Emily's mother because she probably had keys to her parent's house, and Emily probably had keys to the Gaines's home and she just took them."

"That makes sense unfortunately."

She gazed at him. "Now do you understand why this house having a high-end security system seemed to be the better choice?"

"It does seem like we've drawn the attention of the wrong person. Who knew our relationship would be so interesting to anyone but us."

Contemplating her glass, she mused out loud, "I'm trying to understand what this all accomplishes. Yes, it is a little embarrassing to have your personal life brought to the attention of your peers, but it doesn't win the person doing this anything, as far as I can tell."

"Yes it does. *Our* attention."

From a psychological perspective that might make sense, but that was hardly her area of expertise. "I suppose that is true enough." Her smile held a hint of welcome humor. "Maybe you have a secret admirer and that is the woman following me around. Not to inflate your ego or anything, but you are rather attractive."

"Only 'rather'?" He gave her a look of mock outrage, but immediately sobered. "Who knows what is going on?"

"Bailey might. I know I don't. I don't think we can assume it is her."

"If that note is tied to Daniel somehow, or someone else not connected, we'd be wasting his time and muddying the case, but I admit the way the note is phrased is disturbing."

"I think we should tell him and let him judge for himself if he thinks it might be tied into his investigation. Let's keep in mind we aren't necessarily informed on every detail he uncovers."

"I'll concede that point, I guess."

"Tell me why I didn't get out my phone and show Emily that picture of the woman stalking me."

"Probably because she was a young pregnant girl crying right in front of us. I found it distracting anyway." Trey raked his hand through his hair. "That unwelcome thought it might be her has occurred to me too, but why would she stalk you? You are the one, if she is the killer, about to make her dreams come true by doing your best to convict the young man responsible for her daughter being pregnant."

"That I can't answer. It seems more logical she'd come after you, the one likely to get him off."

"Maybe she is by targeting you. Someone knows we are involved on a romantic basis. To strike at me through you would be very effective."

At least he'd used the word romantic. She had no illusions. They were both carefully skirting her impulsive declaration.

I'm in love with you.

She was, she knew it, she just wasn't sure she should have said it out loud.

* * *

He could reveal how alarmed he was by all of this, or remain a cool, calm, analytical man who weighed all the circumstances and made a summary of the facts before any decisions were made.

A try for the latter really didn't work all that well.

Trey asked abruptly, "Can we please just agree to live together here until this is over?"

Stephanie's brows lifted a fraction. "It seems to me we are already sort of doing that."

They were but it wasn't like an agreement or anything. He thought he was usually articulate enough, but searched for the right words. "I mean, like you have clothes in the closet and a cabinet in the bathroom that is just yours for anything you need on a daily basis, so you don't have to run home each evening. Dinner together being a given, not a suggestion one of us makes unless, of course, either one of has something else going on, in which case we tell each other ahead of time."

She clarified carefully. "Like really living together as a couple?"

"I think that sums the idea up nicely. Thoughts?"

Her so-blue eyes were direct. "I guess we can try it until our current predicament is solved and go from there."

He couldn't help but smile because he'd been hoping she'd agree. "I have a housekeeper that comes every Monday."

"Why? You probably use one fourth of the space in this house."

"She dusts the rest."

"You're bribing me."

"No doubt about it, but if you look at it, we both want a child. I am not limited to one. I want a family."

"What are we doing?" She rested her chin on her palm.

"Learning a lot about each other?"

"I'll accept that as an argument."

"I was just making an observation, not an argument."

She laughed. "Okay, I realize that I need to drop the courtroom thing now and then. It's habit, not intentional."

"I find it natural enough, so don't worry about it. Have we come to a conclusion then? You move in and we try it, and see how it goes, especially now, when someone seems to be way too interested in what we are doing."

"If we are viewing it that way, I believe I'd better start dinner and you get to peel the potatoes. Hash browns are my true comfort food and I think that's a fact about me you need to tuck away. Since we are learning about each other and all."

"Duly noted."

But before he did that, he was going to make her do something else. "Dinner sounds great, but I think the best person to ask Emily Gaines if the woman who has been photographed by your neighbor is her mother is Detective Bailey. He actually asked me for the picture and I didn't have it, so I just gave him the tracking device."

"I'll send it to him."

"Do it now. After that I'll peel potatoes."

"I hope you aren't going to be dictatorial on a regular basis." She got out her phone and gave him a quelling look.

"I'll try to keep it in check."

After she pushed a few buttons it was done and sent and then he got the pleasure of watching her in his kitchen, moving with natural grace, her hair against her slender shoulders, answering the occasional question about where something might be that she needed to prepare the meal. He drank his wine and just enjoyed the moment. Beautiful woman fixing him dinner, who could argue with that?

She'd agreed to the live-in proposal. It could be because she really did want to get pregnant, but he hoped it was more because they enjoyed each other — in and out of bed. He was happy with the arrangement. That was not in question.

What was in question was who was taking so much trouble to make them both aware of their observation.

Luckily Bailey didn't call back until they were finished eating, but he was able to provide an answer.

"Yes. That's her. The ex-Mrs. Gaines. Something else happen?"

It was best in his opinion to not dance around it. "You could say that. Besides someone informing her office and my firm that we are together in much cruder terms than that, someone also left a disturbing note on Stephanie's car this evening."

"Read it to me?"

He did.

Silence on the other end. Finally he said, "I think the two of you should be very careful. The suspect's daughter was removed from her care this afternoon until further assessment of the situation and I do have two witnesses that can attest to Jennifer Gaines being unstable, so the harassment deeply bothers me. Having Emily removed might be a trigger. Ms. Gaines isn't fond of me either and Anna has received a threatening phone call from someone because Colin made bail and it was a woman."

"Well, *shit*." Trey muttered the expletive with emphasis. "So, in short, she's certifiable?"

"I used wacko, but off the rails from what I understand."

"Does Anna know?"

"Yeah, she's here."

With Bailey? That was both a relief and interesting. Despite her animosity Trey still cared about her as a person, and he certainly didn't want her in danger. "Well, good, at least she's safe."

"Let me talk to Stephanie. I want her opinion if we have enough to make an arrest. If she thinks so, I'll move forward."

CHAPTER TWENTY-THREE

I'd come to the conclusion I couldn't go home.

Just a poor idea at this stage of the game.

It was fine. I'd seen this coming maybe all my life.

I was truly at loose ends, nowhere to turn and part of it was my fault.

Well, all of it was my fault.

No use to worry about it all any longer.

* * *

He walked out back with the moppet, phone in hand. Chris tended to be aware of his surroundings at all times anyway, but right at that moment, considering he was protecting three people, and four if he included himself, he was more aware than usual. The small back deck seemed secure enough and luckily the backyard was fenced, which meant no leash was required for the dog. She liked to be able to sniff around and was safe, though there was a groundhog that lived under the shed that outweighed her by about thirty pounds, so she steered clear of that if it was out and about. Her tries at friendship had been firmly rebuffed in a manner that was comical and effective.

"What do you have?" Stephanie St. James was sharp and professional as usual. "I understand you don't just want to exacerbate the situation by hauling her in for questioning without enough to charge her. I agree but fill me in."

"I have her prints on both murder weapons, but once again, she could explain those or a lawyer like Austin could. I now have her brother who might testify in court she's prone to violent outbursts, but that's just his word on it. However, three of five victims were related to her in that two of the victims were her parents, and one her ex-husband. She had access to keys to both houses, so that could explain the lack of forced entry. I think most damning is that she's apparently shadowing you and I believe you can thank your neighbor for that picture. I need to be able to arrest her."

Stephanie took a moment but then said definitively, "I think you can. The brother is the key. I know it sounds like a wildcard and it's mostly circumstantial evidence, but I would charge her and I think it would fly. The prints, the keys, the brother and the victims, yes."

"So, murder?"

"You arrest her for murder and we can go from there. I'm in your corner on this one."

"I need to find her first."

"You can't?"

The alarm in her voice was warranted. He informed her, "Jennifer Gaines works at a local real estate office as a secretary and she did not show up for work today. Neither is she answering her phone apparently. I believe you're a target, so just stay with Austin. Lock the doors and secure the windows. I think tomorrow might need to include a mutual trip to work, or maybe work from home?"

"She's on the run?"

"I think she's picked up the scent finally in the air that her actions might run her down. Nothing about how she operates indicates she's a serial killer. She's just someone who loses control and commits murder."

"What does Anna have to say?"

191

"I'm quoting her. I hunt criminals and to an extent know how they operate, but she's the one with a psychology degree."

"Both kids are with you?"

"Yes, they are."

"And Anna? If she decided to remove Emily, she might be the next in line."

As if that hadn't occurred to him. "She'll stay with us."

"Thank you for that. And for the warning."

"Tomorrow I will put together all the resources I have to find our suspect and bring her in and charge her, including the FBI in Knoxville. We will find her."

"I'll inform Hanover of where we are on this."

He ended the call and thankfully was half turned away to go back inside when the first bullet just grazed his shoulder.

Thank you for the warning.

Maybe he should have paid more attention himself.

The second one was a bit more effective as it caught him in the leg so he went backward, staggered and fell. Of course Colin, who might have been the favored target before him was the one who came to the back door and opened it, Emily right behind him. "What the hell?"

"Stay inside but let the moppet in. Don't step out. That's an order." Chris gritted it out, glad he was on the deck and not an easy mark any longer because he wasn't standing, but Colin was tall.

The dog wasn't certain about leaving him there in distress, that was clear and touching but he would be very unhappy indeed if someone shot his dog.

"Go," he told him. "Call the dog."

Another wild bullet hit the glass door with a solid thud.

"Get back! Take Emily."

It hurt, no doubt about it, but he could crawl to the door that they'd left just open enough so he could get in.

No more shots.

Luckily Anna was there. He could stand up so it hadn't broken a bone, but he was bleeding everywhere. He went to sink into a kitchen chair when she rushed into the room and took charge. "Call 911. Tell them two gunshot wounds so the paramedics are ready for it," she ordered Colin as she pulled open drawers until she found a clean towel to compress over the wound on his leg, but Chris could feel the blood soaking his shirt as well.

"I think the bullet went all the way through your thigh which is why you are bleeding so much." She deftly wound the towel around his leg. "With your good hand hold this in place, please, while I unbutton your shirt."

He couldn't help but say, "I've kind of been hoping you would do that someday, but not under these particular circumstances."

She glanced up at him swiftly, a faint smile touching her mouth. "Ditto. Did you see her?"

"Oh God, my mom did this." Emily looked like she might need medical attention more than him. She also sat down in a chair at the table, her face white.

He said in reassurance, "We don't know that. No, I didn't see anyone but there's that line of trees behind the fence. Lots of cover. And needless to say, I wasn't expecting to get shot at on my back deck."

"You didn't get shot at," Anna countered in correction. "You got shot. Twice."

The towel was hardly sufficient and was already wet even though he was putting decent pressure on it. "I noticed that."

"What's the house number?" Colin was on the phone, visibly shaken. "I can't remember."

Emily said, "I do. 123 Olive Street."

"Okay."

Anna gently pulled his shirt open and tugged it off his injured shoulder, which he had to admit looked worse than he expected. The wound was jagged and deeper than the impact had felt. She said to Emily, "Can you get me another towel, please?"

He said dispassionately, "Now I guess I have more circumstantial evidence I can charge her with and the law does not take kindly to assaulting police officers, but then again, I didn't see her either. Maybe one of the neighbors did."

"I can prove she was here from my phone." Emily handed over the towel with a trembling hand. "We have an app on both our phones so she can track where I am at any time. That's how she found this house, I would guess, but it works both ways since our service is shared. I don't know if she realizes I can see where she is too."

Despite that he was in some pain and defiling his kitchen floor with blood, Chris had to register that news with elation. "Are you serious? Where is she now?"

"Let me look."

She took out her phone and in a moment, said, "Driving down this street."

"So I can place her at the scene?" He closed his eyes and blessed whatever power decided to give him a real break. He fought a wince as Anna started to wrap his arm. "I have to say this is turning out to be a pretty good evening."

She looked at him incredulously. "Good? I'm currently kneeling in a pool of your blood."

"I know, but I can really make an arrest now."

"No wonder your girlfriend thought you were too into your job. You don't mind taking two bullets so you can make an arrest?"

"I never said I didn't mind it. I just said since it happened it is a good thing."

"I don't think you are going to be the one making that arrest."

"Like hell I'm not."

* * *

The sound of sirens and flashing lights were both welcome. As a nurse she was unskilled and triage was certainly not her forte, Anna thought in resignation as the responders arrived in force, but she *was* good with handling children.

194

"Stay out of their way and stay in the house." Her voice was firm with purpose. "I think all three of us can agree some loss of control has happened and she's—"

"Really pissed off," Colin finished for her.

"That's one way to put it, but I prefer to say it is very irrational to shoot a law enforcement officer who has no idea you are there and there is no confrontation. I think that's called attempted murder."

"He was hurt because of me." Emily looked stricken.

"No, he was hurt because of *her*. Honey, it is very difficult to acknowledge that adults who are supposed to be responsible individuals make bad decisions. It wasn't your choice, was it?"

"No," she agreed faintly as someone knocked firmly on the door.

She directed Colin and Emily toward the living room. "Just in case, stay clear, please."

The troops arrived in force, coming swiftly through the door and she just pointed them to the kitchen since Chris Bailey was perfectly capable of explaining whatever they needed to know.

To her relief. It could have been a lot worse than two flesh wounds, or so it appeared that way to her.

She could hear Chris protesting he could walk just fine, and losing the argument from the next room, and there was a sinking feeling they would be there alone until a sheriff's deputy appeared in the doorway accompanied by an older man in street clothes.

That was fast.

"Are you Ms. Hernandez?"

"Yes."

"Detective Carter from the sheriff's department. Detective Bailey is my partner, so if you'll give me a moment I'll be back with a few questions and Deputy Stevens here will be staying just to make sure you all are safe this evening."

It never failed to surprise her how much destruction one person could do. Luckily the young deputy looked competent and sturdy and she relaxed a little. She'd still be alert but not alone and unarmed.

"Thank you for that."

His smile was brief and held no humor. "Not a phone call from dispatch I wanted to get. Officer down is never good news. Excuse me."

She certainly did. There was no way he hadn't noted the blood all over her clothes and the medics had refused to let him walk, so Mr. Cowboy might just have to acknowledge he'd been ambushed.

The paramedics won and Bailey was carried out on a stretcher, probably because even though they'd done better than her improvised bandages, he was still bleeding. She was not a doctor, but she thought from the amount of blood maybe the bullet nicked an artery.

The detective who had identified himself as Carter followed them out, but then came back in when the ambulance pulled away. Both Emily and Colin were sitting on the couch and the little dog had chosen her lap for solace, so Anna was sitting in a recliner she suspected a bachelor used for watching television and perhaps slept in now and then.

There was another armchair and Carter chose that and leveled a very businesslike look her way. "Tell me what happened, please."

Under any other circumstance she'd suggest they have a private conversation without children present, but she'd have to have it with them anyway. They'd both been, along with the dog, beyond a doubt traumatized, and the truth be told, she was as well.

"He wanted to talk to Steph — I mean Ms. St. James — about whether or not he had enough to make an arrest that would stick in her opinion — and he went out back to have the conversation, and a few moments later we heard shots. He was hit by two bullets, he got back in the house, we called, and I did the best I could with a limited skill set to repair the damage before other sources trained much better than I am got here."

Carter was nothing like his partner, he thought things over much longer before he asked a question. "No one saw anything?"

"No. There was a third shot, but it just broke the glass door."

"Any idea who thought it was a good idea to shoot a police officer on his back porch?"

"My mother." Emily said it unhappily. "She was here and I'm sure she's mad I ran away."

"And not pleased that I decided it was not a good idea for our organization to return her to the home. Detective Bailey and I discussed how Jennifer Gaines was a prominent suspect in two multiple victim murder cases." Anna said it not defensively but firmly. "I made that decision and most certainly stand by it now. I assume if she could have shot me instead, she would have."

"I think she shot him because he is certainly a more clear and present danger than you, Ms. Hernandez. I agree you made the right decision for the sake of who you represent, but you aren't going to get her convicted of murder, we are." Detective Carter rubbed his jaw. "How do you know she was even here at the time of the shooting? You saw her?"

"My phone." Emily offered it up.

"Your phone?"

She explained about the app and he looked at Anna and said, "Technology changes every single day. I need to keep up."

"Bailey looked at that news with joy even when he was pouring blood on the floor."

"He would."

"Yes, I agree." It was nice be able to smile wryly.

"We needed this."

"No wonder you are partners, you are apparently like-minded."

"Please don't say that to me." Carter looked amusingly pained.

"I happen to think he's quite a smart man."

"Oh, he's intuitive, that is not in question. But alike doesn't apply. I'm going to the hospital now and I will keep you informed if you want me to."

"I would appreciate it."

"Stevens will stay. Until she's apprehended, who knows, so stay alert."

"I believe what just happened and my bloody clothes influence my sense of awareness."

When he left it was the four of them, and truthfully, Anna for once, had no idea what to do. Finally she said, "I'm going to clean up the kitchen floor. Deputy, make yourself at home. If you want a cup of coffee or anything, let me know."

"Yes, ma'am."

The kitchen really was a bloody mess, but before she did anything else, she thought she'd better contact Steph to let her know what happened.

CHAPTER TWENTY-FOUR

If I was done, I'd just think about the bridge over the Tennessee River.
  It was tempting.
  But that feeling had not come over me quite yet.
  Why? I am not sure.

* * *

Anna's text was short and sweet and read: *Bailey was just shot twice and is at the hospital. Pass the information along to Trey, I'm sure you're together.*

Considering Stephanie had just talked to the detective not even an hour ago, she stared at her phone and wordlessly just handed it to Trey. He read it and his expression reflected her own consternation.

"We were on the phone with him not long ago."

"It seems to me he told *us* to be careful." She had to admit she was shocked, but then again, maybe she shouldn't be.

"Anna is there with both Emily and Colin. I have no idea what actually happened, but it seems to me that Jennifer Gaines discovered that they were there and he was in the line of fire. I have no doubt her parents and her ex-husband all knew she was dangerous, but she took them by surprise as well."

"What troubles me is that she has nothing to lose now."

"The alarm system is armed."

"I know." She sighed. "Anna had to add that last bit, didn't she? About us being together tonight. Maybe she did get a note."

His expression was neutral. "I'm sorry but I have to look at it from the same point of view as I did before. We have separate lives. She can't be pissed at me for getting on with mine. I encourage her to do the same. I never did what she accused me of, so I am done with it."

"I think she can be pissed at me because we have been friends for a long time and I am involved with her ex-husband and she hasn't quite yet found peace with the marriage not working out."

"With or without you, it wouldn't have. She and I are too different on a level I didn't recognize in time to stop from making a mistake. She made the same one, so she needs to come to terms with it. I have."

That was probably true, but Stephanie was uneasy she might have been part of the problem and it was difficult to lose a valued friendship.

On the other hand, she agreed with him, so she went back to the original topic. "I assume the sheriff's office would maybe have some information on how severe Chris Bailey's injuries are, and considering our connection to the case, maybe they'll give us some information."

"Detective Carter might be the best source. I have his card."

"Call him?"

"Why do I think, since both of us interact with law enforcement frequently, that he's at the hospital? They work together closely. That's a brotherhood, not just a job. It obviously didn't happen very long ago."

There was a sudden crash right at that moment, followed by the sound of a car alarm.

What the hell?

Stephanie started to rise but he caught her and pulled her down next to him, his fingers locked around her wrist. His voice was firm. "No. Okay, that is probably your car since mine is in the garage. You aren't going anywhere. That's what she wants. It is clear she knows where I live and that you might be here. The car can be replaced, you can't."

He was right, of course, but instinctive reaction had made her want to run out and look.

"This is insane." She just looked at him, listening to the blaring noise.

"She's quite out of control this particular evening, I agree. Insane is an operative word. So is stabbing both of your parents to death while they are sleeping, or shooting three innocent people. Stop trying to make sense of something that will never make sense to either of us. I'm going to call 911 right now and hopefully they can take her in. I doubt my neighbors are enjoying this either."

He was succinct with the person who answered the call. "Here's the address and the person causing the disturbance probably already has shot a police officer this evening so all due caution. Her name is Jennifer Gaines, and she is about to be charged with five murders, so I hope you emphasize the gravity of this situation. She has nothing to lose. Whoever responds needs to understand it is volatile. Send ample backup."

He did have a courtroom presence even under duress, she had to admire how calm and capable he sounded, which really worked for him as a lawyer.

He looked at her when he hung up. "Now I'm going to call Carter."

"I can't deal with this. I'm going to get another glass of wine."

"Don't go into the kitchen. Open a new bottle in the dining room. The kitchen has big windows."

She hadn't even thought of that. Maybe it was the incessant noise reminding her that her car had been vandalized in some way and someone who had murdered people might be waiting for her, so she followed his advice, found the wine cabinet, opened a nice Cabernet and brought the bottle back to the living room.

He was on the phone. "We would appreciate the information, of course."

When he ended the call, she said, "Is he going to be okay?"

Before he could answer someone knocked on the door. "Yes, it sounds like it. Let me go cautiously answer that."

It was her turn. She caught his arm. "No. I want to hear a voice."

"I said cautiously."

"How can you know over the noise of the car alarm?"

There was another sharp rap. "This is Sheriff Lawrence, can you please open the damn door."

She did let go. "That I trust. That's definitely him."

There was no question as she had come across the sheriff in court a time or two.

Trey did lift a brow. "So may I?"

"Yes, and take my keys and have someone turn off that alarm, please."

"My pleasure."

The sheriff was maybe mid-fifties, extremely direct, and reminded her of Hanover since he was also very straightforward. He accepted the keys and a few seconds later the alarm went silent and he came back through the door. He glanced around. "Nice place. Now tell me what's going on here. I was on my way to the hospital when dispatch told me there were calls here at this address, and then Carter called me and said Bailey has been patched up, so I was diverted to talk to you. What the heck is happening?"

The sheriff was casual in jeans and a denim shirt, and no doubt wanted a quiet evening as much as they all did.

Stephanie was straightforward. "We'll fill you in, but my glass of wine is in the living room and Trey really needs to lock that door and reset the alarm. I'm not even going to ask about my car. I'll look in the morning. This way."

She didn't miss that Trey and Sheriff Lawrence exchanged a look that indicated it was easier to just obey an upset woman than argue the point, and normally she would have been amused but the circumstances didn't really allow it.

The truth was, her car was the least of their problems. She went and sat back down, picked up her glass of wine, took a drink, and weighed her words. "Let me sum up this situation. I talked to Bailey earlier, apparently just before he was shot twice, and he and I agreed that he could arrest Jennifer Gaines for five counts of murder in two different cases because of his investigation, and I felt I could charge. However, social services, prudently I might add, chose to remove her daughter from her care, and she has evidently gone off the proverbial deep end. She is out there and doesn't have any brakes when she gets upset, and she's quite upset."

Sheriff Lawrence ran his hand over his face. "If your car is any evidence, she is. Carter said something to that effect but he's a cautious man, and truthfully, he's pretty shook up over Bailey getting shot, so all he told me was Jennifer Gaines was the lead suspect. Where's her daughter?"

"One of your deputies is there with her at Bailey's house."

"Well, that's something. Could this get more complicated? It's one woman. We can contain this. All I have to do is find her."

"I think my car is evidence she's been here quite recently. We heard her smashing the windows but declined to go stop her since she's evidently in the mood to use a gun."

"Carter is tracking her through her phone but it's possible she's just turned it off or ditched it. It isn't showing movement." Not good news.

"I'm of a mind to get the state boys involved in this, so she'd better look out after she shot one of mine. I'll file a report on your car. I think you both should stay here and, yes, keep the alarm on. There doesn't seem to be a lot of question about whether or not she's dangerous."

203

"She's been following me for some reason. My neighbor has noticed her watching my house and took her picture because it was bothering her to have some strange woman lurking around. That's how we know for sure it is her. Her daughter confirmed it to Bailey."

He shook his head and turned to Trey. "There are some nutjobs you just can't understand. Word has it you won't mind at all keeping an eye on Ms. St. James. I'll let you both know when we pick up Jennifer Gaines."

After he departed, Stephanie said wryly, "Let's just make an announcement in the newspaper or on the evening news that yes, indeed, we are sleeping together — oh wait, apparently, there's no need to do that. Word has it?"

"Are you sorry we are? If the answer is no, just ignore it." Trey looked unfazed.

He had a point. She was just unhappy in general on a lot of counts, but probably not as unhappy as the man with two bullet wounds at the hospital. "You're right and no, I'm not sorry. I believe I asked you. I'm just glad Bailey is going to be okay."

"Me too."

* * *

How to analyze the situation was tricky.

Of course Stephanie was unsettled, he was too. It was clear they were targets of some sort, but her in particular?

The vandalism of her car was just pure vitriol. He just wondered if she wasn't being punished because it really seemed clear whoever it was doing all this knew they were together and he was Colin's defense lawyer.

Maybe he needed to warn Senator Grayson he was a potential target as well. He had no idea what Jennifer Gaines knew or to what lengths she'd go. He actually knew very little about her as a person other than it seemed possible she'd murdered five people, and if she'd been a better shot, it might have been six.

"With all due hopes of our well-meaning and competent sheriff finding his quarry, I should inform you, given the events of this evening, I don't own a firearm. My position on that is that unless you are trained to use one — and I can't see any reason I should do that — then why own one."

"I don't either." At least Stephanie gave him a brief smile.

"But I played college baseball. So there is a pretty nice bat in my office, which is right off the dining room if we needed to defend ourselves, but that is the best I can do."

"I could see that baseball player thing." She eyed him, holding her wine glass. "Tall guy, nice wide shoulders and a lean build. What did you play?"

"Pitcher. I was told I had a decent arm, but while I thought about at least trying for pro, I wanted to go to graduate school more than waste my time in the minor leagues waiting to move up. There was no way I wanted to be close to the age I am now, and wondering what I was going to do with the rest of my life because professional athletes are done pretty early — at least they are usually."

"I didn't know that about you."

"What do I not know about you? Give me something."

She tilted her head to the side, thinking about it. "I can speak both Russian and Spanish fairly fluently, and you can toss in some French and Greek. I pick up languages easily for some reason."

That was interesting, but as far as he could tell everything about her fit into that category.

"So you could be a foreign spy." A smile touched his mouth.

"A second career beckons in case my current one doesn't pan out."

"Kind of sexy. Like an erotic novel. *Sleeping with the Spy*. I like the title."

She lifted her brows. "You write it and I'll read it. In the meantime, what are we going to do?"

"Since it has been confirmed she can outshoot us because we have no actual fire power, we will wait until we hear from our good sheriff or from Carter."

"I'm worried about Anna and those children."

"So am I, but at this point, if we went there, it might make it worse. As far as I know, the last attack was on your car in my driveway not very long ago."

"That damage can be fixed."

"Yes it can and I haven't even seen it, but what is she going to do next? She seems fixated on our relationship for some reason."

"It's you. The good-looking competent attorney that might get Colin off fascinates her."

"I disagree." He settled into an opposite chair and just looked at her. "I think she has a girl crush. You're the lovely D.A. who can bury him. She isn't following me and looking in my windows, it's you. She's counting on you and then discovers you are sleeping with the enemy. Let's keep in mind she doesn't think in a linear fashion because murder is an option in her mind."

"As lawyers, I think we are both competent. As amateur psychologists, it is hard to say. I don't know. There's a part of me that wishes I knew what she was thinking, and then again, a part of me that doesn't even want to know because that's a very dark place."

"A valid point."

"This case is going to go south very quickly."

Trey didn't disagree. "It has already. Five people dead, a detective shot, and your car apparently trashed. The pork chops were delicious though, so I'm going to focus on that. Another family recipe?"

"Aunt Jeanne this time." She did laugh. "Are you looking on the bright side of this evening?"

He said softly, his gaze fastened on her, "No, I'm looking at it."

CHAPTER TWENTY-FIVE

I was more than desperate for refuge and it seemed like a good choice.
Besides, I liked the irony of it.
Why not? Turnabout is always fair play.

* * *

Chris wasn't a happy man but it could be worse.

For one thing, he could be dead.

Apparently Jennifer Gaines was not a particularly good shot from any kind of a distance.

It was still galling to have to exit the hospital in a wheelchair and Carter actually have to help him into the car. Despite two gunshot wounds they'd only kept him for a few hours after sutures and bandages, just to make sure the bleeding was stopped.

Nothing critical hit, just flesh wounds mostly and they used locals not a general anesthetic. Though he had a prescription in hand for painkillers, at the moment he didn't feel too bad.

After closing the door, Carter slid into the driver seat and remarked, "So you never saw her."

"Nope. I walked outside because I wanted Stephanie St. James's opinion on whether it would stick if we made an arrest. I really didn't want those two kids to overhear me talking about the murders of their parents because they've been through enough, Emily in particular, not to mention the possible arrest of her mother. I was just standing on the back deck. She had to have been behind the fence."

"According to Lawrence, she then paid Ms. St. James a visit in the form of vandalizing her expensive car that was parked in Austin's driveway."

Chris wasn't all that surprised. "I think Anna Hernandez made the right call removing Emily, but she also set off a shitshow of emotional reaction in an extremely unstable individual."

Carter pulled away from the hospital exit. "That is one colorful way of putting it. Lawrence has decided to bring in the state police on this as well. Everyone is looking for her. I left Stevens to guard Ms. Hernandez and the two minors unfortunately involved in all of this."

"I thought I was doing that, but not well enough it seems."

His partner just remarked diffidently, "As far as I can tell they are fine, you just failed to protect yourself."

"Thanks." Chris gave him an ironic look. His leg did hurt, but the arm was worse for some reason.

"I was shot once in the line of duty. It happens."

The truth was, not often. Most law enforcement officers went their entire career without an exchange of gunfire.

That was new information. "I don't believe you've ever mentioned it."

Carter shrugged. "Why would I? It was when I was in uniform. A domestic call. The abusive husband didn't like me coming to interfere with him trying to beat his wife half to death. He shot me, and I shot him, and we both lived except he got the pleasure of going to jail for quite some time for multiple assault and battery charges."

"Serves him right."

"I couldn't agree more. It hurts like hell, doesn't it?"

"Not an experience I'd care to repeat."

"Go home and take some pain medication and get some sleep."

"She's on the loose and the run. That doesn't make for sweet dreams."

"Lawrence is doing his best to take care of it."

"The state guys might really help." There was no doubt he wasn't at his best because he'd lost quite a bit of blood but not enough for a transfusion thankfully, he was just wobbly to a certain extent. He said slowly, "You know, this might sound strange, but maybe they should check my cabin."

Carter said, "What? It is officially the middle of the night. Why would she go there? I don't even know how to find it in the dark."

"She does because when Austin brought me the tracking device removed from Stephanie St. James car, it was still activated so if she was tracking them, she knows the location. Also, the woman in question is on the run and she's aware I won't be there because she shot me. Safe haven and no credit card needed. Her phone is turned off so we might as well follow my hunch."

"Hunch? Are you serious?"

"I am. I have a feeling."

He could swear Carter sighed. "Not that again. Unfortunately I've been spending too much time working with you and I'm starting to trust that you can think like a criminal. Fine then, I'm fairly sure state troopers would not look there. Shall we head that direction rather than back to your house in town? You aren't exactly in shape to make an arrest, but I sure the hell would like to do it."

"I can't beat her in a footrace through the woods at this given moment but I'm still backup."

"You have one arm in a sling."

"It's my left arm. My gun hand is just fine. If she isn't there, I'll crash on the couch and you can go home and just leave me."

209

"Your gun hand? Who has that? Wyatt Earp?"

"You are the one that keeps making the cowboy comparison, admit it. I'm right-handed, that's all I'm saying. That is how I'd pull."

"I'm making the turn now, so it's decided. I'm assuming if Lawrence knew anything he'd contact me, and the same for Stevens, so maybe your idea has merit."

That they were arguing like an old married couple was kind of amusing, but in truth, Chris did feel like someone who had been shot twice, so he stifled a laugh because it might hurt and hoped he wasn't wasting their time.

The cabin sounded good anyway, since he could count on a good night's sleep there usually. He didn't get that often enough and he needed one. Anna was taking care of the kids and the dog with an officer standing guard, so it would be fine.

Twenty minutes later he found out because there was a car there. He'd dozed off, and he heard Carter mutter, "Really? You were right? I can't believe this. I'm calling Lawrence right now for county backup. Someone is here."

He was able to come awake enough — so much for being backup — to agree. "Do it. I don't want to mess this up. Five murders? And she's already heard us, I promise you. It is very quiet here and I think I can attest to armed and dangerous."

It might be what he liked the most about the place. It was nothing but the utter solitude of it with just the sound of the brush of the wind through the leaves of the trees and the ripple of the river water passing by.

If there was someone inside, they'd heard them pull up.

Carter took out his phone and was already calling in. "This is Detective Carter . . . oh, Darlene? I'm in the boondocks with an injured officer you have the hots for and the property does not have an address as far as I can tell, and please tell the sheriff that we might have found the person he's currently looking for. Have him call me back but warn him my signal is weak."

There was no help for it, Chris had to start laughing, which *did* hurt. "Oh God, only in Tennessee would a detective ever make a call like that."

At least Carter had a sense of humor now and then. "Maybe in Kentucky or even Alabama they might. Come on, give our state a break."

"Maybe. Darlene has the hots for me? Didn't know."

"Don't get too full of yourself. Of course she does because you are young, male, and breathing." Carter slid his weapon free, all levity gone. "This is your property. What's the best approach?"

"There is a back door and if she's smart, she's used it when we pulled up. Let's disable her car before we go inside. Let's face it, she can hide in the woods, but not forever. And if it is her here, she's breaking the law by trespassing, so we can add that to the arrest because I'm not happy if a murderer is in my cabin or even maybe sleeping in my bed. I want her charged for that."

"That sounds reasonable. We can take her in for that at least. Illegal bed sleeping."

"And five counts of murder."

"Let's not forget shooting a police officer. Let me go look at her car. I can see the license plate is covered up for some reason or I'd just run it and we'd know it was her."

"Probably a wise call on her part. Wacko but not dumb."

"I'll be right back. Hopefully we will have assistance soon. I want this by the book."

Considering Carter wanted everything by the book, that wasn't news.

He wasn't at his finest, but Chris opened his door and was only halfway out of the car when their suspect came straight out the front door of the cabin, gun extended.

He hadn't called that right.

Dark hair, jeans and a flannel patterned shirt, her face twisted into a fierce expression of displeasure. "What the fuck are you doing?"

Carter was Carter and polite to a fault, but he did have his weapon leveled. "Ma'am, I'm a detective with the—"

211

She just shot him.

Even Chris was taken off guard by that drastic action and when she swung around toward him, it wasn't conscious thought, he just pulled his sidearm and he used it.

They fired at about the same time.

Luckily, he was better at it than her.

Dead on. She went down before she could fire again.

He didn't really care about her at that point, the evening had been such a disaster. He hobbled over to Carter, who was on the ground, breathing, but it was coming out in gasps. "Hold on. We already know backup is coming. I'm calling 911 right now anyway."

He was with phone in hand but his left arm was in a sling, so it wasn't really all that easy.

"I don't think it is too bad." Carter sat up, clutching his chest. "How could we both be shot by the same woman in one evening?"

"Yeah, it does make you wonder about our abilities as police officers. Just stay quiet."

"What about her?"

"I'm a lot more worried about you, let's put it that way. I think I might have solved all her problems."

"She's dead?"

"I don't know. It doesn't seem to me she's moving much."

Or at all.

He'd worry about that later. Hopefully Carter got as lucky as he did and it didn't hit anything crucial.

Damn his leg hurt but he did bother to go over and kick her gun out of the way with his good one just in case, but he had to admit to a lack of concern over her well-being.

* * *

Stevens got the call, but then wordlessly handed his phone over to her after a few moments of just listening.

"Anna?"

It was Bailey. She was staying awake only by sheer will and a pot of coffee she'd made after rummaging through his kitchen and finding a small pantry with all the necessary items. He was fairly neat for a bachelor, she'd give him that much.

It was a relief to hear his voice.

"Are you still at the hospital? They keeping you overnight?"

"They released me. I'm actually back at the hospital. How are the kids and the moppet?"

What did that mean? She wasn't quite sure how to interpret that statement.

"Colin and Emily are fine and asleep. The moppet is at my feet . . . can you clarify *back* at the hospital?"

"It's a long story and I know it is really late and to be honest, I'm pretty tired myself—"

"Considering how much blood I mopped up off your floor because you were shot twice, I can only imagine."

"Thank you for handling things there. It has been an interesting evening. I'll fill you in later." He rang off.

She handed back the phone and Stevens said calmly, "I guess Carter took a bullet too. He's in surgery."

It was impossible to not just stare at him. "What?"

The young deputy wasn't as detached as he was trying to pull off. "Yeah, I know, right. It's hard to have an officer down, much less two."

"Did he say what happened?"

"Just that the problem was solved."

She had the feeling she and Stevens were forming the same kind of bond soldiers in trenches were legendary for this night. "What does that mean?"

"I'm guessing they made an arrest, but I don't know."

"Two detectives got shot the same night?"

He cupped his hands around a coffee mug that had a U of Tennessee logo on it. "It sounds that way."

"How?"

"Ma'am, bad people are pretty much all we deal with. Why are you in charge of two children who both have murdered parents?"

A valid point.

"True."

* * *

Chris sat in the waiting room where his partner had sat for him earlier, and when Sheriff Lawrence walked in, he was grateful.

Get it over with.

Lawrence was always eloquent. "Been one hell of a night?"

"I think that sums it up."

"I think it is apparent you paid attention in firearms."

"However you look at it, she'd already shot me and also my partner. Are they going to take issue with that in Internal Affairs?"

"No. The good news is Carter went down, but he saw it all. And she'd shot him too fairly point blank, so there you have it."

"The problem is I have to tell her daughter I killed her mother."

"Son, just tell her fortunately you were the better shot."

"Hmm, maybe Anna Hernandez can help me do better than that. This young pregnant girl is staying at my house."

"And her mother tried to kill you."

"She really did but, now that child is an orphan. Part of which is her mother's fault."

"*All* of which is her mother's fault." Lawrence didn't give an inch, his expression implacable. "You're wearing a white hat in my line of vision. Look, in all my time in law enforcement, I have never had officers shot in the line of duty more than once, and never two the same evening. Some people are just bad news."

It was true and he knew it, but telling Emily was a different story.

"I don't know how to explain this."

"Then don't. That child totally understands what she's dealt with all her life. You have no idea what she's been

214

through. If you want to say you are sorry that it happened like it happened, then go ahead because we all are. Anything else isn't necessary. It was going to go that way. We had to stop her and you did."

"I know I'll go through an inquiry." Man, was he tired, the waiting room smelled like stale coffee and he hurt more than a little, but not enough to really complain about it. He didn't have surgery.

"All fatal encounters between law enforcement and civilians require that, yes."

Two nurses in scrubs walked by chatting companionably, the world at work as usual, the hospital busy unfortunately at this hour.

"Son, you've had one of the roughest nights ever and it is four in the morning." Lawrence stood. "I'm taking you home because you look like hell. I'll come back and I will keep you informed."

"Carter stayed for me."

"He hadn't been shot twice then, had he? This is not a request but an order."

Put that way, he didn't have a lot of choice.

When he walked into the house, Stevens was on the couch, half asleep in the modest living room, but aware enough he knew someone had come in. He sat up and pointed. "She's in there, the kids together in the second bedroom. You okay?"

The proper response might have been that he'd been shot twice, his partner had also been shot, and he'd been involved in a fatal shooting with a suspect, but it seemed far too complicated for this time of day, so he just said, "I'm fine. I'm going to change my clothes since these are covered in blood, and go to bed."

"I'll be here."

"Thanks."

He could have pointed out there was really no need, since Jennifer Gaines was no longer on this earth, but he really didn't want to think about it.

215

It was nice to be able to put on a clean T-shirt and boxers and brush his teeth, and Stevens was right, Anna was nicely sleeping in his bed, relaxed with her dark hair glossy in the light of a full autumn moon giving illumination through the window.

He settled next to her and she didn't move at first until she became aware someone had joined her.

She rolled over. "Oh."

"Don't mind me. You are so safe from any overtures of a sexual nature. I'm really tired and have two bullet wounds. Can we just share a bunk? It'll be like summer camp."

"I'm the one that took your bed." She smoothed his hair back with a languid hand and laughed. "Yes to the sharing. I'm tired too."

He'd hoped for a reaction similar to that. "Tonight just sleep and maybe sometime in the future explore other options when we next bunk in together?"

"Perfect."

That was the answer he'd hoped he'd hear.

EPILOGUE

Two weeks later

Senator Grayson met them at a very nice hotel in Nashville where he'd reserved a table in a part of the restaurant clearly reserved for private parties. Trey escorted Stephanie to where he sat, well aware she turned heads in a very form-fitting black dress as they walked through the lobby.

He introduced them. "Senator Grayson of Tennessee, this is Assistant District Attorney Stephanie St. James."

The senator had stood politely, and he accepted her hand. "I believe you are the one who charged my son with three counts of murder."

Her eyes widened and she went very still. "*Your* son?"

No disclosure on his part. Trey had never told her.

She recovered after a moment and sent a swift accusatory glance his way. "I am. I am also the one who didn't want to charge him in the first place and the charges were dropped."

"It sounds like a fair call, since the actual perpetrator was caught." He did look relieved. "Have a seat and let me buy you a drink."

Trey pulled out her chair and seated her and then took one himself. A very aware and discreet waitress appeared and

Stephanie ordered a glass of wine. He wouldn't have minded a nice glass of bourbon like the senator was drinking, but he opted for the same with lighter alcohol content. He was driving.

"How are Detective Bailey and Detective Carter? Both still recovering well, I hope. Good men, both of them, and I hope that the fatal shooting will not blow up all over Bailey."

Stephanie shook her head. "I can't see that happening. Not only had she shot both of them, but it was dark, she was illegally on his property, and she's clearly linked to the other murders by physical evidence. A hearing, and that's it. A clear case of self-defense."

"Good to hear." Senator Grayson took his glass, set it down, stared at it for a moment and then looked at Trey. "This is extremely personal and why I asked you to meet me. My wife is now well aware of the situation."

So he'd decided to just be honest about it. Granted it was a gamble, but sometimes the adage was true, that was the best policy.

"For Colin's sake, given the circumstances, I'm glad to hear that." Trey was hardly qualified to advise the man on his marriage, so he tried to stay noncommittal.

"What are my rights? Do I have any? A simple DNA test can prove I'm his father."

It was a good question. "Family law is not my provenance but considering no one else is responsible for him at this time, I'm sure you do have a say in his life for the time remaining until he turns eighteen."

"What about the girl and the baby? That's my grand-child and as I understand it she's orphaned as well now. They are so young, they can't handle this with no one else to provide assistance. I want him to go to college and we'd be willing to help her as well."

He was starting to get the picture about the request for this meeting, though he was sure Stephanie was having some trouble because she didn't know the backstory.

"You'd actually like custody of them both?"

"If I can give my wife the baby she never could have and both of those kids a decent future, yes. It seems like something that might be good for everyone. You know Colin better than I do. Not permanent custody, but maybe a shared arrangement in which we can help until they are ready and able to take care of the child."

It sounded like a reasonable solution to him. Anna could offer good advice.

"I can talk to them both for you, of course, if that's what you'd like."

"My sense from my single encounter with Colin was that he seems to trust you. He calls you Trey and he calls me sir." His smile was wry.

"We've had more interaction and he is a polite kid."

"Yes, Roxanne did a good job." His voice was tinged with regret. "I'm hoping to keep that legacy going."

"I know Emily has an aunt and uncle but she'd prefer to be with Colin would be my guess. I'm not at all a social worker but I do know one that knows both of them and their circumstances. She can help."

"Social services would not be necessary if they just come with us."

"You have a point about the baby. I don't see how they could take care of it from a fiscal standpoint right now since neither of them really has any resources or a home, so if they could be together, finish high school, and then look forward if that is what they want to do, that would be best in my mind."

"It is worth a try and my wife is very much hoping they'll agree."

It was an interesting conversation to be having with Stephanie sitting there and listening to the exchange since her desire for a baby was not a secret, at least to him. Trey said, "I'll do what I can."

"From a legal standpoint, they probably just don't have a say right now, being minors." Stephanie added to the conversation. "But Colin will soon. However, it has been made clear to me anyway, that he is a good student, and wants to go to college. I'd guess he'll decide it is a good solution to his so suddenly disordered life. Yes, you are a stranger essentially, but so are foster parents."

The senator replied, "I'm going to cautiously say we seemed to connect well enough. Let me know how it goes. What both of those kids have been through . . . I can't imagine."

It was true. At the moment Trey was grateful for his relatively serene and secure childhood. No murdered parents, and no parents that were murderers.

Lucky him.

Fifteen minutes later Senator Grayson excused himself for a meeting which was why he was in Nashville and they were left alone in their exclusive corner. Stephanie considered Trey over the table. "Care to fill me in? I've come to some conclusions, but there are some gaps. So, Colin is his son but not with his wife obviously?"

It was hardly a breach of ethics when the man had told her himself. "He had an affair."

"I've figured that out."

"He took financial responsibility but without having a deep discussion, I am under the impression he does love his wife, they are childless and it is obviously not his problem, but hers. She had multiple miscarriages. He did give me that personal information."

"That would be devastating then to find out another woman had his child."

"It makes me think quite a lot of her that she was able to get past it, and a lot of him that he was able to tell her finally because he cares about his son. Just so you know, there are no secret children on my part."

She smiled. "Or mine."

"I believe I know that already."

"I'm late."

* * *

It was a nice venue with a beautiful view of the city and quiet music in the background, the understated elegance a reflection of the probable price.

He caught himself in time — she saw it, before he asked late for what.

Trey looked gorgeous in his open-necked white shirt and dark slacks, and his expression was priceless. "What?"

"Have we not been having unprotected sex? This is what I hoped would happen, but did not expect so soon." Patiently but with a hint of humor she added, "You do realize it really takes just one time."

"Yes, I understand biology. Have you taken a test?" His dark eyes were intense.

"It's just a few days but I'm extremely on time usually and the tests are pretty sensitive so yes, I did. Yesterday."

"Positive?"

"If it wasn't, would I be telling you this?"

"You're pregnant." He looked incredulous.

"Trey, we'll see how this goes. There's always a chance of a false positive or a miscarriage. I'm taking this one day at a time. Should the situation remain the same, I'll go see my doctor and we will know."

He regrouped, she could see him take it in and gather himself. "I guess I didn't know I'd have such a visceral reaction if it happened."

She'd have been fine if he hadn't reached across the table, taken her hand and lifted it to his mouth in a gallant gesture to kiss her fingers.

Instant tears welled and she wasn't emotional like that usually.

That spoke volumes more than a pregnancy test.

"Let's see how it goes, shall we." Her voice was barely a whisper.

"Steph, you're happy, aren't you?" He looked suddenly uncertain.

"Very. It scares me a little."

"I'll be there every step of the way, as much as you want anyway."

It hadn't occurred to her when she approached him it might be just what he wanted too, she'd just hoped he would agree to help *her* make it happen.

Not that she objected.

"I think I've made it clear you can do as much or as little as you want to be involved."

"I love you and this is my child too. I'd like to make it clear I'm very involved."

He had a point there.

Then he asked, "Should you be drinking that glass of wine?"

At least that made her laugh rather than cry. "One glass of wine isn't a problem. I think I've only drunk half of this one anyway."

I love you.

Well, she'd said it to him.

He gazed at her, his expression serious. "Can I put an argument out there for you to consider?"

"Of course. You can always make one and I will always consider it."

"If this is true, can we make this living arrangement more permanent? One of those spare bedrooms would make a good nursery. I'm thinking the one directly across the hall from the master bedroom."

He was truly serious.

She wasn't sure what response to make but she did know what she wanted to do.

* * *

Chris walked out of the formal interview relieved more that it was just over and he could lose his tie than anything else.

He wasn't happy he was involved in a deadly shooting, but on the other hand, he hadn't initiated it either.

Luckily it was agreed his reaction was reasonable and correct under the code of conduct, so he walked clear of being charged or reprimanded.

Considering he'd been shot twice himself and Carter had some significant damage and that it was probable she'd killed other people, he thought that was fair. He'd returned fire, but just done it better than her.

He still didn't like it, but it had happened.

Anna met him downtown at a café, and he appreciated the time she took out of her day.

"It went fine." He slid into the booth and grimaced. "Well, as fine as anything when you are questioned about a deadly shooting."

She was drinking iced tea and looked cool, reserved, and professional. "I thought it would go that way, because, please, she tried to kill you and also Detective Carter and look at the other people who have suffered because of her actions. She was a very unbalanced woman."

He smiled at her across the table. "Every time I think this is a reasonable world, I'm proved wrong."

"Today it was."

"I'll roll with that. I'll just be happy to be back on duty."

"You were on medical leave anyway for being shot twice."

"I'm more than ready to go back, though Colin and I did spend a lot of time at the cabin and Emily came on the weekends. That was nice."

"Her aunt and uncle are doing their best to try to give her some stability. They're well aware of what she had to deal with her whole life. It didn't bother her to go to the place where the shootings took place?"

Chris didn't think it did. "Don't underestimate how relieved she is to be free of her mother, so no, it didn't seem to as far as I could tell, and she and Colin got to be together."

She considered him. "How about you?"

He shook his head. "If there had been a different decision I could have made, maybe, but there wasn't an alternative. No, I'm fine."

"So, speaking of those two. . . a certain person associated with Colin wants to offer custody of both him and his pregnant girlfriend. It might be the perfect solution because while Emily's aunt and uncle are willing to help her, they are busy people and the news she was expecting wasn't all that welcome."

He made an educated guess. "Grayson? Good for him."

She gazed at him. "That's the one."

"I'm glad for them both. A young man should know his father."

Anna looked at him curiously, her dark hair an arc against her smooth cheek. "You just said that like you have a story."

"Don't we all?"

Maybe someday he'd tell it.

THE END

ALSO BY KATE WATTERSON

DETECTIVE CHRIS BAILEY SERIES
Book 1: THE LAKE HOUSE
Book 2: THE WOODS AT DUSK

Thank you for reading this book.

If you enjoyed it please leave feedback on Amazon or Goodreads, and if there is anything we missed or you have a question about, then please get in touch. We appreciate you choosing our book.

Founded in 2014 in Shoreditch, London, we at Joffe Books pride ourselves on our history of innovative publishing. We were thrilled to be shortlisted for Independent Publisher of the Year at the British Book Awards.

www.joffebooks.com

We're very grateful to eagle-eyed readers who take the time to contact us. Please send any errors you find to corrections@joffebooks.com. We'll get them fixed ASAP.

Made in the USA
Las Vegas, NV
11 March 2022

45479043R10135